Where Every Road Leads Home
Where Every Neighbor is Family

"This book is a work of fiction. While the character and their journey were inspired by the spirit and creativity of a real individuals, the story, characters, and events contained within are entirely products of imagination and are not based on real life. This narrative was created with the assistance of artificial intelligence."

By Richard Dell Schwarz

Forward

To My Dearest Esmeralda,

This book, and every story within it, is for you.

With each passing day, my love for you grows deeper, richer, and more profound. You are the steadfast heart of our home, the quiet strength in every challenge, and the vibrant joy in every triumph. Your kindness, your spirit, and all the countless things you do, big and small, fill my life with an immeasurable happiness.

Thank you for being you, for your unwavering support, and for making every moment an adventure. You inspire me, you complete me, and I cherish every single day we share.

With all my love,

Richard

Table of contents

Contents

1: Rio Seco Rhythms

The air in Rio Seco hung thick and heavy, a syrupy blanket of humidity that clung to everything, including Esmeralda "Esme" as she carved a silent, rolling path through its familiar, sun-baked streets. Seventeen years old, and already possessed of a spirit that chafed against the slow, predictable rhythm of her South Texas town, Esme found her liberation on wheels. Her lime green roller skates, a vibrant slash of color against the muted browns and ochres of the late 1970s landscape, were less an accessory and more an extension of her very being. They were her wings, her silent steed, her passport to a world that, for now, was confined to the cracked asphalt and dusty sidewalks of Rio Seco.

The late afternoon sun beat down with an oppressive intensity, the kind that made mirkorns shimmer in the distance and the asphalt itself seem to sweat. Even the ever-present buzz of cicadas felt muted, as if they too were wilting under the heat. Yet, for Esme, the warmth was an old friend, a constant companion that merely amplified the freedom she felt with every push of her skate. The distant, tinny thrum of a disco beat, filtering out from an open window somewhere, was the soundtrack to her solitary explorations. It was a sound that promised glamour, excitement, a world far removed from the quiet predictability of her days.

Her skates weren't just about speed, though she could certainly fly when the mood struck her. More importantly, they were her vantage point. From her low-slung perspective, the world unfolded in a unique way. She saw the intricate patterns of cracks in the pavement, the determined weeds pushing through them, the faded advertisements peeling from weathered shopfronts. She saw the way Mrs. Gable's prize-winning petunias always drooped by mid-afternoon, the hasty way Mr. Henderson swept his porch each morning, the precise angle at which Sheriff Brody parked his patrol car outside the diner. These were the details, the small observations, that filled her mind, a constant stream of data processed through the filter of her youthful, observant gaze.

Rio Seco was a town built on routine, on the predictable ebb and flow of daily life. But for Esme, that routine often felt like a cage, albeit a comfortable one. Her internal monologue, a constant companion on these solitary rides, was a testament to this yearning. She'd imagine herself on the open highways, the wind whipping through her hair, leaving the familiar streetlights and sleepy houses far behind. She'd picture bustling cities, vibrant with energy, a stark contrast to the languid pace of her hometown. These were not just idle daydreams; they were explorations of a future she was determined to carve out for herself. Her skates, in a way, were already taking her there, mile by rolling mile, through the humid South Texas air.

The sheer kinetic energy of her movement was a defiance against the stillness that threatened to engulf her. As she glided past the weathered storefronts of Main Street, past the sleepy porch swings of the residential areas, she was a blur of motion, a fleeting presence that underscored the static nature of the town. Her parents, bless their hearts, saw her skating as a harmless pastime, a way to get out of the house. They didn't quite grasp the profound sense of agency it afforded her. It was in those moments, with the wind at her back and the rumble of her skates a familiar song, that she felt most herself, most alive, and most free.

The late afternoon sun cast long, distorted shadows that danced and wavered with her every turn. She'd often find herself drawn to the edges of town, to the places where the neatly paved streets gave way to gravel and then to dusty, rutted tracks. It was here, on the periphery, that the true character of Rio Seco began to reveal itself, the veneer of small-town charm peeling back to expose something a little more raw, a little more untamed. Her skates navigated these rougher terrains with a practiced ease, the slight wobble of the wheels over loose stones a familiar challenge, a test of her balance and her resolve. She was a cartographer of her own small world, charting its hidden paths and forgotten corners, all from the saddle of her rolling freedom.

Her mind, as always, was a restless thing. While her body moved with practiced grace, her thoughts were a whirlwind of possibilities, questions, and observations. She'd analyze the subtle shifts in people's expressions as she passed them, cataloging their moods, their worries, their fleeting joys. Was that a new worry line etched on Mrs. Gable's brow, or was it just the way the sun was hitting her face? Did young Timmy really drop his ice cream, or was he deliberately trying to get his mother's attention? These were the silent narratives Esme was perpetually constructing, piecing together the invisible threads that connected the lives of the people in Rio Seco. Her skates, in this sense, were her research tools, allowing her to observe without being intrusive, to witness without being a part of the immediate scene.

She remembered a time before the skates, a time when her world was confined to the short walks between home, school, and the occasional visit to the town square. It felt like a lifetime ago, a period of subdued existence when her spirit felt coiled and restricted. The moment she'd strapped on her first pair of skates, a rather clunky, borrowed pair that had left her ankles aching for days, something had shifted. It was as if a locked door had creaked open, revealing a new dimension to her existence. The lime green ones, a birthday gift she'd practically wept over, were the culmination of that newfound freedom, a symbol of her independence and her growing confidence.

The heat, while relentless, also served to dampen the usual sounds of the town, creating a hushed anticipation. It was as if the entire community was holding its breath, waiting for something to break the monotony. Esme felt it too, a subtle undercurrent of… something. It wasn't necessarily a bad feeling, more like a prickle of awareness, a heightened sense that the usual rhythms were about to be disrupted. Perhaps it was the quietness that seemed to settle over the town more deeply than usual, or the way conversations seemed to end abruptly when she skated by, as if people were guarding their words a little more closely.

She often wondered what lay beyond the familiar horizons of Rio Seco. The faded, sepia-toned photographs in the town's small library offered glimpses of a past she couldn't quite connect with, a more formal era that seemed a world away from the burgeoning trends of the late seventies. She devoured magazines, particularly those that featured faraway places and glamorous lifestyles, absorbing the images of cities alive with neon lights and the hum of constant activity. These vicarious experiences fueled her desire to break free, to carve her own path, even if, for now, that path was paved with cracked asphalt and traced by the wheels of her skates.

Her observational skills, honed by countless hours of solitary cruising, were sharp. She noticed the subtle nuances of human interaction, the unspoken language of body posture and fleeting glances. She saw the shy way young Billy Peterson looked at Sarah Miller across the aisle at the grocery store, the nervous fidgeting of her father when he talked about the upcoming property taxes, the way her mother's smile never quite reached her eyes when she spoke about her own unfulfilled dreams. These were the raw materials of life, the unspoken stories that Esme absorbed, even as she glided past, a silent observer in the grand theater of Rio Seco.

The hum of the distant disco music, growing slightly louder as she neared the town square, was a siren song of sorts, a promise of a different kind of life. It spoke of Saturday night dances, of flashing lights and synchronized movements, of a world where inhibitions were shed and joy was unashamed. Esme often imagined herself there, not just as a spectator, but as a participant, her skates abandoned for dancing shoes, her observant gaze replaced by the exhilaration of movement. But for now, the roller skates were her dance floor, the streets her ballroom, and the rhythm of her wheels the only music she truly needed.

She rounded a corner, the familiar scent of honeysuckle and exhaust fumes filling her nostrils. The town square, with its ancient oak tree and the slightly crooked bandstand, was a focal point of Rio Seco life. It was where the annual Fourth of July picnic was held, where the Christmas tree was lit, and where, on any given day, you could find a microcosm of the town's social dynamics. Today, however, there was a subtle quietude, a hush that felt out of place even for the sleepy afternoon. A few people milled about, their conversations subdued, their gazes often drifting towards the empty pedestal in the center of the square.

Esme's internal monologue, ever present, began to churn. What was it about the square today? It was more than just the heat, more than just the usual lull of a weekday afternoon. There was a palpable sense of something missing, a void that even the omnipresent Rio Seco sunshine couldn't quite fill. Her skates seemed to slow instinctively, as if sensing her own growing curiosity. She paused near the old fountain, its gentle gurgling a familiar, comforting sound, and allowed her gaze to sweep across the scene. Her keen eyes, accustomed to picking out details from a distance, registered a subtle tension in the shoulders of the few townspeople present, a guardedness in their hushed tones. It was a feeling, a premonition, that the usual rhythms of Rio Seco were about to be profoundly disturbed. Her world, built on the steady glide of her wheels, was about to encounter an unexpected bump in the road.

The very air seemed to hum with an unspoken question, a collective sigh of confusion that Esme, with her finely tuned observational skills, couldn't ignore. She felt the familiar prickle of curiosity, the instinctive urge to understand, to uncover the hidden narrative. Her skates, ever ready, responded to her unspoken command, carrying her closer to the heart of the subtle disquiet that had settled over the town square. The journey had truly begun, not with a bang, but with the quiet, insistent hum of her lime green wheels on the sun-warmed asphalt, carrying her towards an unfolding mystery.

The late afternoon sun, though still fiercely hot, had begun its slow descent, casting longer, more dramatic shadows across the familiar landscape of Rio Seco. Esmeralda, her lime green roller skates a vibrant blur against the dusty browns and faded pastels of her small South Texas town, felt the familiar rush of freedom with every push. These skates were more than just a mode of transportation; they were an extension of her will, her gateway to observing the world from a unique, unhurried perspective. As she navigated the humid streets, the distant thrum of disco music, a persistent echo of the era, served as the soundtrack to her constant internal dialogue.

From her low-slung vantage point, the cracks in the pavement were like ancient maps, each fissure telling a story of time and weather. She saw the way Mrs. Gable's petunias, usually so vibrant, were starting to wilt under the oppressive heat, a small tragedy in the grand scheme of Rio Seco life. She noted the precise angle at which Sheriff Brody's patrol car was parked outside the diner, a silent testament to his predictable routine. These were the details that Esme absorbed, cataloged, and analyzed, her mind a restless processor of the mundane, always searching for the subtle nuances that lay beneath the surface.

Her dreams, however, rarely stayed confined to the familiar streets of Rio Seco. They soared beyond the sleepy town limits, chasing the echoes of disco beats and the promise of faraway cities. Her internal monologue was a constant stream of "what ifs" and "somedays," a testament to her independent spirit and her keen observational skills, sharpened by countless hours spent gliding through the quietude. She yearned for a world that pulsed with a different kind of energy, a world where her restless spirit might find a more fitting rhythm. The skates, in this sense, were not just a means of escape, but a symbol of her burgeoning desire for agency, for the power to chart her own course.

The heat was a palpable presence, a thick blanket that muffled sounds and intensified the colors of the landscape — the fiery red of bougainvillea spilling over fences, the deep green of mesquite trees, the pale blue of the boundless sky. Esme's skates, however, cut through this atmospheric haze with an effortless grace, a testament to her skill and her deep connection to the worn asphalt. She felt a kinship with the very ground she traversed, her wheels an extension of her own determination to keep moving, to keep exploring, even when the world around her seemed content to remain still.

The constant, almost hypnotic rhythm of her skates was a form of meditation, a way for her to process the subtle shifts and currents within her small community. She saw the hushed conversations that ceased abruptly as she approached, the furtive glances exchanged between townsfolk, the way certain individuals seemed to carry a weight of unspoken concern. These were the breadcrumbs of a larger narrative, a story that Esme, with her innate curiosity and her unparalleled ability to observe, was beginning to piece together, even if she didn't yet know what that story entailed. The late 1970s in Rio Seco were, for Esme, a period of quiet observation, of gathering threads, of preparing for a journey she couldn't yet fully define, but which her spirit already felt calling. Her skates were the vehicle, her eyes and ears the compass, and her restless heart the engine driving her forward.

The late afternoon sun, a relentless golden hammer, beat down on the checkered asphalt of the Sonic Drive-In. For Esme, the familiar symphony of sizzling burgers, the metallic clang of ice in soda cups, and the tinny, cheerful jingle of orders being placed was the soundtrack to her late shift. Her lime green skates were tucked away in her locker, traded for the slightly worn, white-soled sneakers that offered a different kind of stability on the sticky, oil-scented floor. The air inside was a heady mix of fryer grease, cheap air freshener, and the faint, sweet tang of cherry limeade, a potent cocktail that was uniquely Rio Seco.

Esme navigated the narrow pathways between the parked cars, a tray laden with burgers, fries, and impossibly cold Cokes balanced precariously in her hands. Her eyes scanned the familiar vehicles – the chipped paint of Sheriff Brody's cruiser, the dented fender of Mrs. Gable's avocado-green sedan, the pristine, almost offensively white pickup truck belonging to the mayor's son. Each car was a story, a mobile extension of its owner, and Esme, with her knack for observation, had them all filed away in her mind.

"Hey, Esme, slow down there, buttercup!"

Raul, her co-worker and the undisputed king of sarcastic banter, leaned against the gleaming chrome of a vintage Mustang, wiping down a spilled milkshake with a practiced swipe of his rag. His dark hair was slicked back, a few rebellious strands always escaping to frame his mischievous grin. Raul was the embodiment of Rio Seco's easygoing charm, a guy who could charm the socks off anyone while simultaneously making a snarky comment that would leave you laughing.

"Can't let these hungry customers starve, Raul," Esme retorted, expertly maneuvering around a poodle skirt that had clearly seen better days. The girl wearing it, Brenda Jenkins, was fluttering her eyelashes at a boy in the car next to hers, a young man named Jimmy who Esme suspected had a permanent residence parked in front of the Sonic.

"Just remember," Raul drawled, his eyes glinting, "you're not paid to be a waitress, you're paid to be a miracle worker. These people expect miracles, and you're our resident deity."

Esme just grinned, reaching the Mustang. The driver, a burly man named Hank who ran the auto repair shop on the edge of town, gave her a nod. Hank was a man of few words, but his gruff exterior hid a surprising kindness. He always tipped well, usually with a handful of change and a gruff, "Keep the change, kid."

"One cheeseburger, large fries, and a cherry Coke," Esme recited, her voice clear and steady. She'd memorized hundreds of orders, a mental Rolodex of cravings and preferences. Hank nodded again, his gaze drifting towards the radio, where a fuzzy rendition of "Dancing Queen" was playing. The entire car seemed to vibrate with the familiar melody.

As she walked back to the kitchen, the clatter of skates echoed from the adjacent lot where a group of younger kids were attempting some rather wobbly figure eights. They were the next generation of Rio Seco's roller enthusiasts, and Esme watched them with a mixture of fondness and amusement. She remembered being that young, that eager to master the glide, the turn, the graceful stop.

Back in the bustling kitchen, the air was thick with the steam from the fryers and the comforting aroma of onions. Mrs. Peterson, a woman whose apron seemed permanently dusted with flour, was expertly flipping burgers on the flat-top grill. Her movements were precise, efficient, honed by years of service. She was the matriarch of the Sonic, a quiet force of nature who kept everything running smoothly.

"Esme, honey, that order for the Miller car is almost ready," Mrs. Peterson said, her voice warm and melodic, like the gentle hum of a summer evening. Her eyes, a soft shade of brown, held a knowing sparkle. She'd seen Esme grow up in Rio Seco, had watched her transition from a shy little girl to the independent young woman she was today.

"Got it, Mrs. P," Esme replied, grabbing a fresh set of trays. The Miller car was a regular fixture, always ordering the same thing: two chili dogs, onion rings, and a diet Dr. Pepper for him, a strawberry shake and a side of onion rings for her. Mr. Miller, a nervous accountant, and Mrs. Miller, a woman whose perpetually worried expression never quite softened, were a study in quiet domesticity. Esme often wondered about their lives outside of these predictable Sonic stops.

She delivered the order, handing the plastic tray to Mr. Miller, who fumbled with his wallet. "Keep the change, son," he said, his voice a little shaky. Esme offered a polite thank you, her gaze lingering for a moment on the meticulously organized glove compartment, a tiny glimpse into a world of order she couldn't quite fathom.

The drive-in was a microcosm of Rio Seco, a melting pot of its inhabitants. There were the high school kids, their laughter echoing through the twilight, fueled by hormones and freedom. There were the families, escaping the oppressive heat of their homes for a taste of something cool and sweet. There were the solitary figures, nursing a drink and lost in their own thoughts, finding a silent companionship in the anonymity of the crowd.

And then there were the regulars, the ones Esme knew by name and by order. There was Old Man Fitzwilliam, who always ordered a single scoop vanilla cone, his gnarled hands trembling as he accepted it. He'd sit in his ancient pickup truck, watching the world go by, a silent sentinel of a bygone era. There was the trio of retired teachers who always arrived just before sunset, their chatter a lively mix of gossip and reminiscences. And of course, there was Sarah, the waitress from the diner across town, who often stopped by for a late-night malt, her bright red hair a beacon in the gathering darkness.

Esme found a peculiar comfort in this routine, this predictable flow of faces and orders. It was a canvas upon which she could paint her observations, sketching the intricate social tapestry of her hometown. She'd listen, not eavesdropping, but absorbing. Snippets of conversation would drift over the hum of the cars, fragments of lives lived out in the open air.

"…told him straight, I said if he can't handle the heat, he oughta get out of the kitchen…"

"…saw the strangest thing yesterday, out by the old creek bed, looked like…"

"…don't care what the papers say, this town's not what it used to be, not at all…"

These overheard whispers, these fleeting confessions, were like puzzle pieces, hints of the larger stories unfolding around her. She didn't pry, didn't insert herself, but she stored them away, filing them alongside the precise specifications of a double bacon cheeseburger or the exact number of pickles Mr. Henderson liked on his patty melt.

Her mind, however, was never truly tethered to the immediate. As she delivered a tray of onion rings, her gaze would instinctively drift to the edge of the parking lot, to the dusty road that led out of town, the same road her skates often followed. She'd see the faint glow of the distant highway lights, a silent promise of places unknown, of experiences yet to be had. The conversations swirling around her, the familiar faces, the predictable rhythms — they were all part of the life she knew, but a part of her was always yearning for something more, something beyond the checkered asphalt and the clatter of trays.

There was a young couple in a cherry-red Camaro parked near the back, their heads close together, their hushed conversation punctuated by soft laughter. Esme recognized them as new to Rio Seco, their presence a subtle ripple in the town's placid waters. They seemed to radiate a different kind of energy, a subtle restlessness that Esme recognized and understood. She wondered what brought them here, to this quiet corner of South Texas, and what they thought of its slow, steady pace.

Suddenly, a frantic shout cut through the evening air. "My keys! Has anyone seen my keys?"

It was Mrs. Gable, her voice laced with panic. She was digging through her oversized purse, her face contorted with distress. A small crowd began to gather, a collective concern blooming amidst the casual diner atmosphere.

Esme, her tray momentarily forgotten, scanned the ground around Mrs. Gable's car. Her sharp eyes, accustomed to spotting dropped quarters and stray bottle caps, landed on a glint of metal beneath the driver's side door.

"Mrs. Gable!" Esme called out, her voice cutting through the murmur. "Are they maybe… under your car?"

She skated – no, she hurried, her sneakers carrying her swiftly across the asphalt – and pointed. Mrs. Gable, her face etched with relief, peered down. There they were, her car keys, glinting innocently on the ground.

"Oh, thank heavens, dear!" Mrs. Gable exclaimed, scooping them up. "I don't know what I'd do without them. Or without you, Esme!" She beamed at Esme, a warm, genuine smile that made the slight heat from the kitchen feel like a gentle caress.

Raul appeared at her side, a sympathetic grin on his face. "See? Miracle worker. Told you."

Esme just blushed, a faint warmth spreading across her cheeks. It wasn't about the job, not entirely. It was about being a part of something, about knowing that even in this sleepy town, she could make a difference, however small.

As the sky deepened from a hazy blue to a bruised purple, the neon lights of the Sonic began to hum to life, casting an ethereal glow over the parking lot. The music from the jukebox, now playing a soulful ballad, seemed to slow, mirroring the languid rhythm of the approaching night. Esme found herself leaning against a support pillar, watching the headlights create shifting patterns on the ground, her mind once again drifting.

She saw the way the teenagers flirted, the hesitant touches, the shared laughter, the stolen glances. She saw the way the older couples sat in companionable silence, their shared history a palpable presence. She saw the families, their children's faces sticky with melting ice cream, their parents' faces softened by the day's weariness and the simple joy of a shared treat.

And in the midst of it all, Esme felt a quiet sense of belonging, a connection to the pulse of Rio Seco. The Sonic, with its predictable offerings and its quirky inhabitants, was more than just a place to work; it was a stage, a classroom, a community. Her skates might carry her away to faraway dreams, but for now, her feet were planted firmly on the sticky asphalt, her eyes wide open, absorbing the sweet, sometimes sour, but always compelling symphony of life in her small South Texas town. The sizzle of the grill, the clang of the trays, the distant echo of music – it all wove together into a sonic sweetness, a comforting, familiar melody that, for tonight at least, felt like home. Even as the heat began to recede, a different kind of warmth settled over Esme, the quiet satisfaction of a day spent not just working, but truly *seeing* the world around her. The lingering scent of fried onions and sweet cherry limeade was, in its own way, a promise of the continued unfolding of the stories she was so adept at observing. The rhythmic clatter of trays and the low murmur of conversations formed a comforting backdrop to her ever-present internal narrative, a narrative that was, she suspected, just beginning to gain momentum. The familiar faces, each etched with their own unique story, provided a constant stream of data for her keen observational skills, a living, breathing encyclopedia of Rio Seco's souls. She saw Mr. Henderson painstakingly wiping down his counter, his movements methodical and precise, a stark contrast to the wild, untamed energy of the younger kids attempting cartwheels near the concession stand. It was this contrast, this blending of the old and the new, the mundane and the unexpected, that made Rio Seco, and her job at the Sonic, so endlessly fascinating. Even the usually boisterous Sheriff Brody, who'd stopped in for his usual double bacon cheeseburger, seemed to carry a certain weariness tonight, his shoulders slumping just a fraction more than usual as he handed Esme his payment. She wondered what kind of call had kept him out so late, what unseen currents were stirring beneath the surface of their seemingly placid town. The jukebox, manned by Raul during his breaks, cycled through a familiar rotation of hits, each song a marker of time, a nostalgic echo of summers past and summers yet to come. Esme found herself humming along to a Fleetwood Mac tune, her thoughts drifting to the shimmering highway lights visible from the Sonic's edge, a constant reminder of the world beyond Rio Seco's familiar embrace. Yet, tonight, there was a grounding force at play, a sense of being tethered to this specific moment, this specific place. The shared experience of a hot South Texas evening, the simple act of serving and being served, created a subtle, invisible bond between the people gathered here. Esme felt it, this unspoken camaraderie, this shared humanity that transcended the individual stories playing out in each parked car. She was a part of it, a crucial cog in the gentle, predictable machinery of Rio Seco. As she handed a strawberry shake to a young boy whose eyes were wide with anticipation, she felt a quiet sense of purpose. It wasn't the grand adventure she sometimes dreamed of, but it was real, it was present, and it was hers to observe, to experience, and to understand. The day was drawing to a close, the sky now a deep indigo studded with the first hesitant stars. The Sonic, a beacon of light and sound in the encroaching darkness, continued its steady hum, a comforting constant in the ebb and flow of life. Esme, though tired, felt a familiar surge of energy, the quiet thrill of witnessing the world unfold, one order, one conversation, one passing car at a time. Her lime green skates, waiting patiently in her locker, would soon carry her home, but the sonic sweetness of the Sonic, the symphony of sizzling, clinking, and chattering, would linger long after the last customer had driven away. It was a day in Rio Seco, and for Esme, it was a day filled with the subtle, often overlooked, richness of everyday life, a testament to the fact that even in the most predictable of places, there was always something new to discover, if one only knew where to look, and listened closely enough. The fading echoes of laughter and the receding headlights painted a picture of contentment, a quiet rhythm that Esme found herself increasingly attuned to, each subtle nuance of the evening adding another layer to her understanding of this place she called home. It was a sweet, familiar melody, a sonic tapestry woven from the ordinary moments of life, and Esme, with her keen senses and her restless spirit, was its most dedicated listener. The air, still warm but beginning to carry the faintest whisper of a cooler night, seemed to hold its breath, a collective sigh as the day surrendered to dusk, and the Sonic, with its ever-present neon glow, continued to be the heart of Rio Seco's nocturnal rhythm.

The usual, comforting drone of Rio Seco had begun to fray around the edges. It wasn't a dramatic unraveling, not yet, but more like a subtle dissonance in the familiar melody. Esme, attuned to the town's rhythms from her vantage point at the Sonic, felt it first. It was in the way conversations, usually open and spilling out onto the asphalt like dropped fries, now seemed to shrink and retreat, conversations held in furtive whispers behind cupped hands. It was in the quick, darting glances people cast around, as if searching for something, or perhaps, someone.

The air itself felt different, heavier, as if the oppressive South Texas heat had finally settled into something more sinister than mere discomfort. It was a shift as palpable as the difference between the sticky, oil-scented floor of the Sonic and the cool, smooth linoleum of the county courthouse. Esme, ever the observer, cataloged these subtle changes, filing them away alongside the precise number of pickle slices Mr. Henderson requested.

She'd noticed it a few days ago, a growing quietude around the town square, a place usually buzzing with the afternoon's languid energy. The usual clusters of elderly gentlemen debating the merits of different fishing lures on the park benches were fewer, and their conversations seemed to trail off abruptly when anyone new approached. Mrs. Gable, usually a fixture at the bakery, ordering her weekly lemon meringue pie with a cheerful flourish, had been in and out in a hurried blur, her eyes wide and unfocused, offering only a clipped "Just the usual, dear," before practically fleeing the premises.

Then there were the hushed exchanges she'd overheard while clearing tables or delivering orders. Snippets that, individually, might have meant nothing, but strung together, painted a disquieting picture.

"…said he saw something strange, out by the old water tower. Said it wasn't like anything he'd ever seen before…"

"…can't be true, can it? Not here, not in Rio Seco…"

"…they're keeping it quiet, that's what they're doing. Don't want to cause a panic…"

These were not the usual tales of who'd won the church bingo or whose prize-winning watermelon had been sabotaged. These were laced with an undercurrent of fear, a tremor of the unknown that resonated even in the mundane chatter of a small town. Esme found herself straining her ears, her innate curiosity pricked by the sheer strangeness of it all. It was like trying to tune into a radio station that was barely broadcasting, the signal weak and distorted, hinting at something significant but remaining frustratingly out of reach.

The most prominent absence, the one that loomed large in the growing unease, was that of Rex. Rex, the armadillo. Not a real armadillo, of course, but the town's beloved, larger-than-life mascot. Rex, with his perpetually cheerful, somewhat goofy painted smile, his segmented armor crafted from glittering, recycled materials, and his penchant for leading the annual Pecan Festival parade, was as much a symbol of Rio Seco as the dusty plains or the endless blue sky. Rex was a constant, a cheerful, scuttling presence that children adored and adults fondly tolerated.

But Rex was missing.

He wasn't just in for repairs; he was truly, utterly gone. His usual perch outside the town hall, where he served as an impromptu photo op and a silent guardian, was empty. The space where he normally stood, adorned with a rotating display of seasonal decorations, now felt stark and vacant. Esme had first noticed it a few days prior, during her roller skates journey to the library, a route that took her past the town hall. She'd initially dismissed it, assuming Rex had been temporarily moved for cleaning or perhaps a new coat of glitter. But as the days passed and his familiar, if somewhat kitschy, form failed to reappear, a subtle worry began to creep in.

When she'd casually mentioned Rex's absence to Raul during a lull in the Sonic's evening rush, his usual flippant demeanor had faltered, replaced by a flicker of something akin to confusion. "Rex? Yeah, I haven't seen him either. Thought he was getting a touch-up for the upcoming Founders' Day picnic. Mrs. Henderson was complaining about his chipped ear last week."

But Mrs. Henderson, the town's unofficial gossip chronicler and a woman who missed nothing, hadn't mentioned anything about Rex being taken in for work when Esme had served her a cherry limeade earlier that day. Instead, Mrs. Henderson had been unusually tight-lipped, her usual stream of commentary reduced to monosyllabic replies, her gaze fixed on something beyond Esme's shoulder, towards the increasingly quiet town square.

The silence surrounding Rex's disappearance was as unsettling as the whispers themselves. There were no official announcements, no posters tacked to the community bulletin board announcing his temporary relocation. It was as if Rex, the very embodiment of Rio Seco's communal spirit, had simply vanished into thin air, and no one was talking about it, or at least, not openly.

Esme found herself piecing together the scant fragments of information, her mind working like a detective's, sifting through the mundane details for any hint of significance. The unusual activity near the old water tower, mentioned in hushed tones. The hurried visits to the bakery, the averted gazes. The general air of disquiet that had settled over the town like a sudden, unexpected fog. And now, the missing armadillo. It felt connected, a thread weaving through the subtle shifts in Rio Seco's predictable tapestry.

She tried to engage her younger cousin, Leo, who worked part-time at the hardware store near the town square, but he'd been equally evasive. "Rex? Nah, haven't seen him, Esme. Busy, you know? Lots of people buying gardening supplies. Must be that heat wave everyone's talking about." But Leo's eyes had darted away nervously, and his hands had been clasped so tightly his knuckles had turned white. He knew something, or at least, he'd heard something that made him uncomfortable.

Even the normally unflappable Sheriff Brody seemed to carry a new weight. Esme had seen him the previous evening, parked in his cruiser outside the town's only diner, the lights of the Sonic casting a faint glow on his grim profile. He'd been on his radio, his voice low and urgent, too low for Esme to catch the specifics, but the tone was one of concern, not the usual calm authority he exuded. He'd glanced her way as she'd skated past, a brief, almost imperceptible nod, but his eyes held a weariness that went beyond a long day.

The absence of Rex, the town's cheerful, scuttling mascot, felt symbolic. It was as if the town's very spirit had been misplaced, its usual warmth and openness replaced by a creeping apprehension. Rex, made from discarded hubcaps and shimmering soda can tabs, was a testament to Rio Seco's resourcefulness and its quirky, down-to-earth charm. His disappearance felt like a tear in the fabric of their collective identity, a silent, unsettling omen.

Esme leaned against the cool metal of the Sonic's order board, the scent of onions and fried dough a familiar comfort in the midst of her growing unease. The distant rumble of a truck heading out of town, a sound usually lost in the evening's symphony, now seemed amplified, a lonely punctuation mark in the deepening silence. She watched the stars begin to prick through the darkening sky, each one a tiny, distant light, and wondered what shadows were growing in the heart of Rio Seco, what whispers were being carried on the wind, and what had happened to their beloved, missing armadillo. The usual rhythms of the drive-in, the clatter of trays and the murmur of conversations, continued around her, but Esme felt a growing detachment, her senses now focused on the subtle tremors beneath the surface, the first faint signs that the predictable, comforting melody of Rio Seco might be changing.

The loudspeaker, usually reserved for announcing daily specials or the occasional lost child's name, crackled to life with an official announcement that sent a fresh ripple of unease through the already tense air of Rio Seco. Mayor Thompson's voice, normally booming with an almost theatrical enthusiasm for town events, was strained, devoid of its usual warmth. "Citizens of Rio Seco," he began, his words amplified and slightly distorted, echoing off the brick facades of the downtown buildings, "it is with a heavy heart and a profound sense of disappointment that I must inform you of a regrettable incident." He paused, and Esme, who had just finished delivering a double cheeseburger and fries to a pickup truck parked near the edge of the Sonic lot, felt a knot tighten in her stomach. She knew, with a certainty that chilled her despite the lingering heat, what was coming. "Our beloved mascot, Rex, the Rio Seco Armadillo, has been... removed from his customary place outside the town hall."

The announcement, delivered with such solemnity, confirmed what many had only dared to whisper about. Rex, their Rex, the shimmering, slightly gaudy testament to Rio Seco's unique brand of charm, was gone. Not misplaced, not undergoing a secret renovation, but truly, irrevocably *gone*. The implications hung heavy in the air, thicker than the scent of frying onions. Rex wasn't just a statue; he was a landmark, a gathering point, a source of shared pride and gentle amusement. He was the mascot that had presided over every Pecan Festival, every Founders' Day picnic, every school parade for as long as anyone could remember. He was woven into the fabric of Rio Seco's collective memory, a constant, glittering presence. His absence was a void that felt personal to every single resident.

As the mayor's words faded, a murmur swept through the town square. Conversations that had been hushed and furtive moments before now erupted into a cacophony of shocked exclamations and bewildered questions. People emerged from shops, their faces etched with disbelief and a nascent anger. The usual rhythm of the afternoon – the gentle hum of commerce, the occasional passing car, the laughter of children – was shattered, replaced by a collective gasp of dismay. Esme, her roller skates still on, felt an almost magnetic pull towards the epicenter of this sudden unrest. The town hall. That's where the loss had occurred, and that's where the questions would undoubtedly begin.

Skating with a newfound urgency, Esme navigated the milling crowds. Her route took her past the bakery, where the door was propped open, a few people clustered inside, their voices hushed and urgent. Mrs. Gable, usually so effusive, stood near the counter, her face pale, her usual rosy cheeks drained of color. Esme saw her nod grimly at something one of the other patrons said, her hand pressed to her mouth as if to stifle a cry. The hardware store, usually a hub of activity on a Saturday afternoon, had an unusual quietude about it; even Leo, her cousin, usually quick with a sarcastic quip, was nowhere to be seen, the door to the back room firmly shut. The general store, too, seemed to be experiencing an exodus, with folks drifting out onto the street, drawn by the news.

She reached the town hall, a stately, if somewhat weathered, brick building that normally exuded an aura of quiet authority. Today, however, it was the focal point of a collective bewildered grief. A small crowd had gathered on the manicured lawn in front of it, their eyes fixed on the stark, empty space where Rex should have been. The concrete pedestal, usually adorned with Rex's triumphant, if slightly chipped, grin, now stood bare, a monument to his sudden absence. The morning dew had long since evaporated, but a faint dampness still clung to the concrete, as if the absence itself had wept.

Esme, ever the observant one, circled the perimeter of the scene, her eyes scanning the ground with a practiced intensity. While others milled about, sharing theories and lamenting their loss, Esme was looking for the details, the subtle clues that might have been overlooked. She noticed it almost immediately, a series of scuff marks on the concrete, roughly circular, as if something heavy and perhaps awkwardly shaped had been dragged. These weren't the clean, deliberate marks of a forklift; these were rough, jagged abrasions, interspersed with faint skid marks, suggesting a struggle, or at least, a forceful removal.

Her gaze swept further, taking in the surrounding area. The grass bordering the sidewalk was trampled in places, more than could be explained by the usual foot traffic. It looked as though vehicles, or perhaps something large and unwieldy, had been maneuvered there. Then, her eyes landed on something small and glinting near the edge of the pedestal, half-hidden by a clump of ornamental grass. Crouching down, her roller skates making a soft whirring sound on the pavement, she reached for it. It was a small, tarnished metal button, the kind that might have once adorned a sturdy work jacket or perhaps a military-style coat. It seemed out of place in the generally tidy surroundings of the town hall. She picked it up, turning it over in her fingers. It had an unusual insignia pressed into its surface, a stylized raven with its wings spread. She'd never seen anything like it before.

As she continued her silent, methodical examination, Esme's attention was drawn to the faint but distinct impressions left in the soft earth beneath a nearby oak tree. They were tire tracks, unlike any she recognized. They were narrower than the tires of a typical car, and the tread pattern was unusually deep and aggressive, as if designed for off-road conditions. The tracks seemed to lead away from the town hall, disappearing into a dense patch of mesquite bushes that bordered the edge of the park. It was as if a vehicle, or perhaps something

on wheels, had come to a halt there, and then made its hasty departure in the direction of the highway, or perhaps, deeper into the surrounding countryside.

The official announcement had only confirmed what many had suspected. Rex wasn't just missing; he had been *taken*. The casual disappearance of a beloved, albeit quirky, town mascot was hardly plausible. The whispers, the unease, the furtive glances – it all began to coalesce into a more sinister narrative. This wasn't a prank. This was something else, something deliberate and, Esme suspected, something far more significant than anyone in Rio Seco was ready to admit. The tarnished button, the unusual tire tracks, the scuff marks – they were pieces of a puzzle, and Esme, with her sharp eyes and insatiable curiosity, felt an undeniable urge to try and fit them together. She slipped the button into her pocket, the cool metal a tangible reminder of the mystery that had suddenly descended upon her quiet town. The rhythm of Rio Seco had been disrupted, and the silence left by Rex's absence was deafening, pregnant with unspoken questions and a growing sense of apprehension.

The mayor's pronouncement, delivered with a gravity that felt entirely out of place for a missing armadillo, hung in the air like the oppressive heat of a summer afternoon. It confirmed the growing unease, solidifying the vague sense of disquiet into a palpable certainty: Rex was gone, stolen. But for Esme, the shock quickly morphed into something else, a potent cocktail of indignation and a fierce, almost primal, need to understand. She wasn't one to stand by and watch her town suffer, especially not when the culprit was likely lurking just beyond the visible horizon. Her roller skates, usually a means of efficient transit for her Sonic deliveries, suddenly felt like instruments of destiny, her wheels primed to roll towards answers.

The crowd around the town hall was a kaleidoscope of worried faces, each person contributing to the low murmur of speculation. Theories were exchanged in hushed tones: a rival town's prank, a collector of oddities, even something more outlandish involving extraterrestrials. Esme, however, found herself less interested in the wilder conjectures and more attuned to the physical evidence she'd already glimpsed. The scuff marks, the misplaced button with its peculiar raven insignia, the unusual tire tracks — these weren't the hallmarks of a casual jest. They spoke of intent, of planning, of a calculated act. And Esme, with her sharp eyes and an analytical mind honed by years of piecing together customer orders and anticipating their needs, felt a distinct tug, a quiet insistence from within, urging her to take these disparate pieces and weave them into a coherent narrative.

She wasn't a detective, not by any official definition. Her resume boasted no training in forensics or criminal investigation. Her expertise lay in remembering complicated orders, navigating the busiest shifts at Sonic with grace, and offering a friendly, if slightly reserved, smile. But beneath that unassuming exterior lay a core of fierce determination, a refusal to accept injustice or confusion when clarity was within reach. This was her town, her community, and Rex, in his own kitschy way, was a part of its identity. His disappearance left a hole, not just in the town square, but in the collective spirit of Rio Seco. She couldn't just skate away from that.

The decision, once it solidified, felt less like a choice and more like an inevitability. She pictured herself weaving through the streets, her skates a silent blur against the asphalt, piecing together the clues the authorities might overlook. She imagined the thrill of discovery, the quiet satisfaction of connecting the dots, of bringing a sense of order back to the chaos. The thought sent a shiver of anticipation through her, a feeling far more exhilarating than simply waiting for the mayor to make another announcement. This was an opportunity, a chance to prove that even a young woman with a part-time job and a penchant for roller skates could make a difference.

Her first instinct was to return to the scene of the crime, the now-empty pedestal outside the town hall. The crowd was still there, a solid mass of bewildered citizens, but Esme managed to weave through them with practiced ease. The roller skates were, in this instance, a significant advantage, allowing her to glide past clusters of people without disrupting their conversations or drawing undue attention to herself. She approached the bare concrete base, her eyes immediately drawn to the scuff marks. They were more pronounced than she remembered in the dimming afternoon light, deeper gouges in the concrete, evidence of significant force. She knelt, her skates balanced precariously, and traced the rough edges with her fingertip. This wasn't a simple tug-of-war; it was a deliberate, forceful removal.

Her gaze swept over the surrounding grass. The trampled area was more extensive than she'd initially assessed. It wasn't just a few disturbed blades of grass. It looked as if a vehicle, or perhaps a heavy piece of equipment, had been maneuvered precisely into this spot, then likely turned sharply. She tried to visualize the scenario: the slow, careful approach, the securing of Rex, the jarring movement of extraction, and then the hasty retreat. The sheer weight of the armadillo, a solid fiberglass structure, meant that whatever had been used to move him was substantial.

The button. She reached into her pocket, her fingers closing around the small, cool metal disc. She pulled it out, examining it again under the waning sunlight. The raven insignia was still clear, sharp despite the tarnish. She turned it over, looking for any identifying marks, any manufacturer's name, anything that might provide a lead. Nothing. It was a mystery in itself, a small, silent testament to the anonymity of the thief. She thought about where such a button might come from. A uniform? A specialized piece of clothing? It felt too robust, too utilitarian for everyday wear. It suggested a purpose, a specific context.

The tire tracks, too, occupied her thoughts. She remembered their unusual narrowness, the aggressive tread. They weren't the kind of tires you'd find on a standard sedan or even most trucks. They looked more like something you'd see on an all-terrain vehicle, or perhaps a military-grade jeep. And they led away, towards the dense mesquite bushes that hugged the edge of the park. That was her next logical step. If the perpetrators had made their escape in a vehicle, the tracks would be the most direct path to follow.

As the crowd around the town hall began to disperse, with people heading home to discuss the day's events over dinner, Esme felt a surge of urgency. This was her window of opportunity, a brief period before the authorities might secure the area more thoroughly, potentially obscuring the very clues she was trying to decipher. She pushed off from the pedestal, her skates gliding smoothly across the pavement. Her destination was the edge of the park, the place where the tire tracks disappeared into the thorny embrace of the mesquite.

The mesquite bushes formed a thick, almost impenetrable barrier, a tangled mass of branches and sharp thorns. Esme slowed as she approached, her senses on high alert. The ground here was softer, the earth less compacted than the paved areas. It was here that the tire tracks should be most visible, and also, potentially, most vulnerable to being erased by wind or subsequent activity. She scanned the ground meticulously, her eyes adjusting to the dappled shade cast by the dense foliage.

There they were. Fainter now, but undeniably present. The narrow impressions, the deep grooves of the tread pattern, were etched into the dry earth. They led into the thicket, suggesting that whatever vehicle had been used had driven directly into the dense undergrowth, a bold, or perhaps desperate, move. Esme knew that pushing her skates through that terrain would be impossible, even dangerous. But she could still follow on foot, carefully stepping where the tracks indicated.

She dismounted her skates, tying them securely to her belt loop. The unfamiliar sensation of walking on the uneven ground was a stark contrast to the fluid motion of skating. Her boots, designed for urban streets and Sonic aisles, felt clumsy and ill-suited for this task. Still, she pressed on, her eyes fixed on the ground, her focus absolute. The tracks led her deeper into the mesquite, the thorns snagging at her jeans, the dry leaves crunching underfoot. It was slow going, a stark reminder of the physical challenges that investigative work could entail.

She reached a small clearing within the mesquite, a space where the branches had been pushed aside, almost as if something large had forced its way through. And there, on the ground, was another piece of evidence. A small smear of what looked like grease or oil, dark and viscous against the pale earth. It was fresh, too fresh to have been there long. It suggested a mechanical issue, perhaps, or a hasty, clumsy repair. She resisted the urge to touch it, knowing that any contamination could compromise its integrity. She committed its location to memory, noting its proximity to the tire tracks.

As she continued her slow progress, Esme's mind raced. Who would steal Rex? And why? The button with the raven… it felt significant. She imagined a group, organized, equipped with a vehicle capable of traversing rough terrain, and dressed in attire that might feature such distinctive buttons. This wasn't a solo operation. This was a planned extraction. The sheer audacity of it was staggering.

The mesquite eventually thinned out, giving way to a more open scrubland that sloped gently downwards towards the highway. The tire tracks continued, leading in that direction. Esme paused, a growing sense of apprehension mixing with her determination. The highway represented a departure, a move towards anonymity, towards leaving Rio Seco behind. She had to make a decision. Following the tracks onto the highway would be incredibly dangerous, especially without a clear objective.

She looked back towards Rio Seco, the familiar outlines of the buildings softened by the approaching dusk. She could almost hear the worried conversations, the uncertainty that now permeated her town. She thought of Rex, the stoic, somewhat ridiculous armadillo, a symbol of their shared identity. He deserved to be found. And she, Esme, was the one who had the nascent clues.

She decided to return to the town square, to gather her thoughts and perhaps find a different approach. The immediate pursuit on foot seemed too perilous and potentially fruitless if she didn't have a clearer idea of where she was going. The greasy smear and the tire tracks were valuable pieces, but they needed to be contextualized. She needed to think, to strategize. Skating back through the streets, the roller skates once again her reliable companions, she felt a renewed sense of purpose. Her investigation had officially begun, not with flashing lights and official pronouncements, but with a quiet resolve, a pair of roller skates, and a pocketful of unanswered questions. The rhythm of Rio Seco might have been disrupted, but Esme was about to inject a new beat into its unfolding mystery. She felt a quiet thrill, the kind that comes from stepping into the unknown, from embracing a challenge that resonated with her very core. The case of the missing armadillo was now her case, and she intended to see it through to the end.

2: Clues on the Cruising Lanes

The Rio Seco sun, a relentless orb even as it dipped towards the horizon, cast long, distorted shadows across the familiar streets. Esme, her roller skates a blur against the asphalt, felt a different kind of urgency now, one born not of a grand pronouncement, but of a quiet, persistent plea. Mrs. Gable, her usually stoic neighbor, had been in tears earlier that afternoon, her voice quivering as she described the inexplicable absence of Mittens, her ginger tabby. Mittens, a creature of habit, never strayed far, and his vanishing act was as baffling as it was distressing for the elderly woman.

"He always comes for his saucer of cream at precisely four o'clock, Esme," Mrs. Gable had explained, dabbing at her eyes with a lace-trimmed handkerchief. "He's never missed it. Not once in his twelve years."

Esme, despite the lingering adrenaline from the Rex incident and the gnawing questions about the raven button and the tire tracks, couldn't refuse. Mrs. Gable's distress was a familiar ache, a testament to the interconnectedness of their small town. So, she'd traded the thrill of the chase for the quiet pursuit of a missing feline, her skates now a tool for a different kind of search.

Her route took her through the residential backstreets,
areas she rarely traversed during her Sonic deliveries.
These were the quiet zones, the hushed pockets of Rio
Seco where life unfolded behind manicured hedges and
securely latched garden gates. She skated with a gentle
hum, her senses tuned to the slightest rustle, the
faintest meow. She peered into shadowy alleyways,
their corrugated iron fences adorned with graffiti that
seemed almost quaint compared to the mystery of
Rex's abduction. She checked under porches, behind
overflowing bins, her gaze scanning the dappled
sunlight filtering through the leaves of ancient oak
trees.

It was in one of these less-traveled alleyways, a narrow
passage between Mrs. Henderson's prize-winning rose
garden and the crumbling brick wall of the old cannery,
that Esme's routine search took an unexpected turn.
The air here was thick with the scent of damp earth
and something metallic, a faint, almost imperceptible
odor that snagged at her awareness. She was mid-turn,
her skates gliding silently, when she heard them.

Voices. Low, guttural, and distinctly out of place.

She instinctively slowed, her body leaning into a subtle
pivot that brought her to a near standstill behind a
towering stack of discarded wooden pallets. The sound
was muffled, as if emanating from beyond the brick

wall, but the words, though fragmented, were chillingly clear.

"...can't believe it was that easy," one voice rasped, a gravelly undertone suggesting a smoker or someone with a perpetually sore throat. "Thought the old dinosaur would put up more of a fight."

Esme's heart hammered against her ribs.

Old dinosaur? Could they be talking about Rex? The fiberglass armadillo, while undeniably an icon, hardly qualified as a dinosaur, but the context felt unnervingly relevant.

"Quiet," the second voice hissed, sharper, more urgent. "Anyone could hear you. We just need to get him to the rendezvous point. No slip-ups."

Rendezvous point. These weren't casual pranksters. These were people with a plan, individuals who considered Rex a prize to be moved. Esme's mind raced, piecing together the fragments. They had taken Rex, and their method, whatever it was, had been surprisingly straightforward for them. The mention of a "rendezvous point" solidified her suspicion that this was a coordinated effort, a pre-arranged transfer.

She strained her ears, trying to catch more. The voices grew fainter, as if the speakers were moving away from the wall, their steps muffled by the soft earth on the other side.

"...the transport will be waiting by the old quarry road," the raspier voice continued, his tone laced with a note of anticipation. "They're paying good money for… unusual acquisitions."

Unusual acquisitions. The phrase sent a shiver down Esme's spine. It confirmed her hunch that Rex wasn't just a mascot to these individuals; he was a commodity, something valuable enough to be stolen and transported. The old quarry road. That was miles out of town, a desolate stretch of land known for its abandoned limestone pits.

The second voice responded, a low murmur that was swallowed by the ambient sounds of the town. Esme waited, her muscles tensed, but the voices didn't return. The alleyway was once again filled only with the distant drone of traffic and the rustling of leaves.

She remained frozen for a long moment, the information settling over her like a heavy cloak. This was more than just a local dispute or a bizarre prank. This was organized crime, albeit of a uniquely peculiar nature. The casualness with which they spoke of stealing Rex, of "unusual acquisitions," was disturbing. It implied a network, a demand for the bizarre.

Her mission to find Mittens had inadvertently led her to a crucial piece of the puzzle. Her agility on skates, allowing her to navigate these forgotten spaces, had paid off in a way she hadn't anticipated. She hadn't found the ginger tabby, but she had stumbled upon a conversation that offered a glimpse into the minds of Rex's abductors.

With a deep breath, Esme pushed off from the wall, her skates finding their rhythm again. The alleyway seemed to hum with a newfound significance. She continued her search for Mittens, but her focus had shifted. Every shadow, every rustle of leaves, now carried a potential double meaning. She kept her eyes peeled, not just for a missing cat, but for anything out of the ordinary – an unfamiliar vehicle, a discarded item, anything that might connect back to the overheard conversation.

She emerged from the alley onto a quiet residential street, the late afternoon sun painting the houses in warm, golden hues. She spotted Mittens a few minutes later, perched regally atop Mrs. Gable's garden shed, nonchalantly grooming his ginger fur as if he hadn't caused a moment's worry. Esme couldn't help but smile, a mixture of relief and amusement washing over her. She called out to him, and with a surprisingly agile leap, the tabby landed at her feet, nudging her hand with his head before trotting off towards his waiting saucer of cream.

Back at her own small apartment, the adrenaline from the overheard conversation still coursed through her veins. She needed to process what she'd learned. The quarry road. The rendezvous point. The talk of payment for "unusual acquisitions." It all pointed to a deliberate, organized theft.

She pulled out her worn notebook, the one she used for Sonic orders and important reminders. She flipped to a clean page, her pen poised.

"Two unfamiliar individuals. Heard them in alley behind Henderson's garden. Mentioned 'old dinosaur' (Rex?), 'easy to take'. Talked about rendezvous point by old quarry road. Payment for 'unusual acquisitions'. Transport waiting."

She reread the notes, her brow furrowed in concentration. This wasn't enough to go to the authorities with, not definitively. A hushed conversation overheard in an alley could be dismissed as hearsay, misinterpreted ramblings. She needed more concrete evidence. The raven button and the tire tracks were her physical clues. This conversation provided a potential destination and a motive.

Esme knew her next move. The quarry road. It was a long shot, a potentially dangerous one, but it was the only lead she had that pointed away from Rio Seco. She needed to understand who was behind this, and why they would steal their town's beloved, albeit kitschy, armadillo.

She strapped on her skates again, the familiar feel a comforting anchor in the swirling uncertainty. The sun was beginning to dip below the horizon, painting the sky in vibrant shades of orange and purple. It was the perfect time for a discreet excursion. She wouldn't be able to skate all the way to the quarry road; it was too far, too treacherous for her skates. But she could get closer, use her skates to cover the initial miles quickly and quietly, then perhaps find another mode of transport if needed, or scout from a distance.

As she glided out of her apartment complex, the sounds of evening settling over Rio Seco, Esme felt a flicker of something akin to excitement. This was no longer just about finding Mittens or returning Rex out of civic duty. This was a genuine investigation, a test of her own resourcefulness and courage. The cryptic conversation, the tangible clues, the sheer audacity of the crime – it all coalesced into a mystery that was far more compelling than any Sonic delivery route. She was no longer just Esme the Sonic girl; she was Esme, the investigator, rolling towards the unknown, her path illuminated by the fading light and the growing certainty that she was on the right track. The curious case of the runaway feline, while resolved, had inadvertently opened the door to a far larger, far more intriguing enigma.

The fluorescent lights of the Sonic cast a sterile glow, a stark contrast to the fading twilight outside. Esme, her roller skates shed and tucked under the counter, was back in her element, the familiar scent of fries and cherry limeades a comforting backdrop to the buzzing undercurrent of her mind. The overheard conversation in the alleyway replayed itself, each word a thread in a growing tapestry of suspicion. The quarry road, the rendezvous, the talk of 'unusual acquisitions' – it was more than just chatter; it was a blueprint for something illicit. She served a vanilla cone to a giggling group of teenagers, her movements efficient, her smile practiced, but her ears were far from idle. The diner, usually a hub of predictable teenage drama and local squabbles, had suddenly transformed into a potential intelligence hub.

She leaned against the counter, ostensibly wiping it down with a damp cloth, her gaze sweeping across the booths and tables. Each patron was now a potential source, a unwitting informant. Mr. Henderson, perpetually clad in his worn fishing vest, was holding court at his usual corner table, regaling anyone who would listen with an elaborate, and frankly improbable, tale about a giant catfish he'd supposedly encountered in the Rio Seco river. Esme tuned him out, his boisterous voice usually a constant, but today it faded into the background hum. Her focus was on Mrs. Gable, who was sharing a quiet cup of tea with a friend, her face etched with a lingering sadness, her conversation a hushed lament about Mittens' uneventful return. Esme felt a pang of guilt for her own preoccupation, but the larger mystery of Rex's disappearance felt like a weight too heavy to ignore.

Then there was Mark, a perpetually bored high school senior who sometimes worked the night shift here. He was currently slumped in a booth with a couple of friends, their laughter a little too loud, their gestures a bit too expansive. Mark had a reputation for knowing everyone and everything that went on in Rio Seco, a self-proclaimed connoisseur of local gossip. He was a primary target for Esme's eavesdropping. As she refilled a nearby table's drinks, she caught snippets of their conversation.

"…no idea where he is, man. My dad said the whole police force is out looking," Mark was saying, his voice laced with a feigned nonchalance that didn't quite mask a glint of something else in his eyes – curiosity, perhaps, or something more guarded.

"They think it was kids, right? Like, a senior prank gone too far?" one of his friends chimed in, their voice muffled by a mouthful of onion rings.

Mark shrugged, a slow, deliberate movement. "Could be. But who'd steal the damn armadillo? It's just… weird. And the way it disappeared. No signs of forced entry at the park, no broken fences. Like it just… walked off."

Esme's internal antennae perked up. 'No signs of forced entry'. That contradicted the tire tracks she'd seen near the park, tracks that suggested a vehicle had been involved, not a leisurely stroll. Unless, of course, the perpetrators had been clever enough to conceal their method of entry. Or, perhaps, Mark's information was incomplete, or deliberately misleading. The word 'weird' hung in the air, a small acknowledgement of the sheer absurdity of the situation, but Esme felt it was an understatement. This was beyond weird; it was organized.

She continued her circuit, clearing tables, collecting empty cups, her movements a practiced dance that allowed her to drift within earshot of various conversations without appearing overly interested. She overheard Mrs. Gable's friend, a kind-faced woman named Carol, offering hushed condolences to Mrs. Gable. "It's just awful, Agnes. Rex was such a fixture. I can't imagine who would do such a thing. Especially with the Founder's Day parade just around the corner."

Founder's Day. That was only a week away. Rex was the undisputed king of the parade, leading the procession through the heart of Rio Seco. His absence would be a gaping, armadillo-shaped hole. Esme filed that information away. The timing was significant. Was the theft a preemptive strike, designed to disrupt the town's most cherished event? Or was it merely coincidental, a opportunistic crime that happened to fall before the parade?

She moved towards the service counter, ostensibly to restock napkins, her path bringing her close to a booth occupied by two men in work boots and faded jeans, their faces etched with the weariness of a long day. They were local contractors, known for taking on whatever jobs came their way, from minor repairs to larger construction projects. Their conversation was low, almost conspiratorial.

"…heard they're offering a decent reward for information," one of them said, his voice a gravelly murmur. "More than enough to make it worth someone's while to talk."

"Yeah, well, what good is information if you can't back it up?" the other replied, taking a long swig of his soda. "I'm not sticking my neck out for some fiberglass critter unless I know it's safe. Besides, wouldn't surprise me if it's some out-of-towners. Always looking to stir up trouble."

Esme lingered, pretending to sort through a stack of plastic lids. 'Out-of-towners.' That aligned with the overheard conversation about a 'rendezvous point' and 'transport'. It suggested an operation that extended beyond the borders of Rio Seco. The mention of a reward was also noteworthy. It indicated that the town council, or whoever was responsible for Rex's well-being, was taking the theft seriously. But who would

know about a reward if it hadn't been publicly announced yet? Or perhaps they were simply speculating, hoping for a reward.

Her gaze drifted back to Mark and his friends. Mark had pulled out his phone, scrolling through something with a focused intensity. He seemed to be privy to more than he was letting on. Esme made a mental note to try and engage him in conversation later, when the diner started to thin out. He was a known quantity, a reliable source of information, albeit one who often embellished his tales.

She remembered the raven button. It had felt out of place, a small, dark anomaly against the backdrop of Rex's peeling paint. She'd picked it up, a tangible piece of evidence, and now she wondered if it belonged to one of the men she'd overheard, or perhaps to someone connected to them. The conversation had mentioned 'unusual acquisitions,' and a raven button, while seemingly insignificant, could be a marker, a calling card, for a particular group.

The tire tracks were another puzzle piece. They were distinct, a specific tread pattern that Esme's keen eye had registered. She'd seen similar treads on vehicles before, but where? It was a fleeting memory, a frustrating whisper at the edge of her consciousness. She needed to recall where she'd seen that pattern, what kind of vehicle it belonged to. It was a detail that could place a specific vehicle, and by extension, a specific person, at the scene.

As the evening wore on, the diner slowly emptied, the boisterous laughter replaced by the low hum of the air conditioning and the occasional clatter of dishes from the kitchen. Mark and his friends were getting ready to leave. Esme saw her chance.

"Hey Mark," she said, leaning casually against the counter as they passed. "Rough night out there, huh? Everyone's talking about Rex."

Mark paused, a flicker of something unreadable crossing his face. He glanced at his friends, then back at Esme. "Yeah, man. Crazy. Hope they find him."

"Me too," Esme said, keeping her tone light. "You hear anything interesting? You always seem to know what's going on." She offered a friendly, disarming smile.

Mark hesitated, then a slow grin spread across his face. "Well, you know how it is. People talk. Some say it was those new guys who moved into the old Miller place out on the edge of town. Always keeping to themselves, never come into the diner."

"The Miller place? That's pretty isolated," Esme commented, feigning casual interest. "What kind of guys are they?"

"Don't know, exactly," Mark admitted, shrugging. "Kind of quiet. Saw one of them once, driving a dark colored truck. Big tires. Looked… serious, you know?"

'Dark colored truck. Big tires.' That description fit the tire tracks. Esme's mind raced. This was a potential lead, a tangible connection between the vehicle and a person. "And they're new in town?"

"Yeah, moved in a few weeks ago," Mark confirmed, starting to walk away. "Anyway, gotta bounce. Tell your boss I said hi."

Esme watched him go, her mind a whirlwind of new information. The new residents at the Miller place. A dark truck with big tires. It was a thread, a fragile one,

but a thread nonetheless. She made another note in her mental ledger.

She looked around the mostly empty diner. The late-night crowd was sparse, mostly tired locals seeking a final caffeine fix. She overheard a brief exchange between two regulars, their conversation about the stolen armadillo laced with a grim sort of humor.

"Fifty bucks says it's up in pieces by now, ready for the scrap heap," one of them grumbled, stirring his coffee.

"Nah, too valuable to scrap," the other countered. "Someone's got a plan for it. Always happens when there's a big event coming up. Someone wants to make a statement."

'Make a statement.' What kind of statement? Was this a political protest? A personal vendetta? Or was it simply about money, about the 'unusual acquisitions' she'd overheard being discussed? The motive remained elusive, a shadowy figure lurking just beyond the reach of her current understanding.

Her thoughts returned to the quarry road. It was a desolate stretch of land, an abandoned industrial site that had become a haven for teenagers looking for a place to party or explore. It was also a perfect place for a clandestine meeting, a place where people could come and go without being noticed. The 'transport waiting' mentioned in the alley conversation could easily be waiting there.

She thought about her skates. They were her advantage, her ability to move quickly and quietly through the town's less-traveled paths. The quarry road was a significant distance away, too far for a casual skate, but she could use her skates to cover the initial miles, to reach a point where she could perhaps find another way to get closer, or at least scout the perimeter.

The more she pieced together, the more she realized this wasn't a simple case of vandalism or a prank. The coordinated nature of the theft, the talk of rendezvous points and payment, the potential involvement of an unknown group from outside of town – it all pointed to something more organized, more sinister. She felt a strange mix of trepidation and exhilaration. The mystery of Rex's disappearance had evolved from a local curiosity into a genuine investigation, and she, Esme, the Sonic delivery girl, was at its forefront.

She began to tidy up, wiping down the last of the tables, her mind already racing ahead, planning her next move. The quarry road was calling, a siren song of secrets and potential danger. She needed to gather more tangible evidence, something that could connect the overheard conversation to the tire tracks, to the raven button, to the new residents at the Miller place.

She considered the possibility of going to the police, but the thought of presenting her fragmented clues — an overheard conversation, a raven button, and a vague description of a truck — felt inadequate. They would likely dismiss it as youthful fantasy, the ramblings of a girl too immersed in detective novels. She needed something concrete, something irrefutable.

As she locked up the Sonic for the night, the streetlights casting long, eerie shadows, Esme felt a renewed sense of purpose. Her initial concern for Mittens had inadvertently set her on a path that was far more significant, far more dangerous. She had stumbled upon a hidden current beneath the placid surface of Rio Seco, a current of illicit dealings and shadowy figures. The missing armadillo was no longer just a symbol of town pride; it was a key, unlocking a door to a mystery that was only just beginning to unfold. The whispers in the alley, the gossip in the diner, the tangible clues she'd collected — they were all pieces of a puzzle, and she was determined to assemble them, no matter the cost. The quarry road awaited, and Esme, with her skates and her sharp eyes, was ready to roll towards whatever secrets it held. She stepped out into the night, the cool air a welcome embrace, her mind already charting a course, driven by the insatiable need to uncover the truth, one overheard whisper at a time. The ordinary had become extraordinary, and Esme was ready to embrace the challenge.

The air at the Rio Seco park, even in the hushed pre-dawn light, still thrummed with an unsettling stillness. It was the kind of quiet that felt charged, as if the very air held its breath, waiting for the truth to reveal itself. Esme, having traded her Sonic uniform for a more practical, darker ensemble that blended with the shadows, felt the familiar hum of anticipation that always preceded a deep dive into a mystery. Her roller skates, her trusted companions in navigating the winding paths of Rio Seco, felt perfectly balanced beneath her feet as she glided onto the damp grass where Rex, the beloved fiberglass armadillo, had last stood.

The initial reports had been frustratingly vague: Rex was gone. No witnesses, no immediate signs of a struggle, just an empty pedestal where the town's proud mascot should have been. But Esme knew that absence itself was a clue. She began her methodical sweep, her eyes, trained by countless hours of observing the comings and goings at the diner, scanning the ground with an almost surgical precision. The dew-kissed grass offered little immediate insight, but it was the subtle disturbances, the almost imperceptible alterations to the landscape, that Esme sought.

Her skates moved her in a slow, deliberate circle around the now-bare concrete base where Rex had been bolted down. The morning mist clung to the ground, softening the edges of everything, but Esme's gaze was sharp, piercing through the veil of moisture. She was looking for anything that didn't belong, anything that spoke of a hurried departure, a struggle, or a calculated removal. The pedestal itself showed no signs of forced entry, no splintered wood or gouged metal, reinforcing the perplexing nature of the disappearance. It was as if Rex had simply dematerialized.

Then, as she completed another pass, her left skate catching slightly on an uneven patch of ground, she saw them. Faint, almost ephemeral, tire tracks. They were pressed into the soft earth at the edge of the paved pathway, leading away from the park's central plaza. Esme knelt, her gloved fingers hovering inches above the impression, careful not to disturb them. Her mind immediately began comparing them to the usual vehicles she saw in Rio Seco: the sturdy pickups of the local farmers, the sensible sedans of the town council, the sputtering engines of the teenagers' beat-up cars. These tracks didn't match any of them.

The tread pattern was distinctive, a series of aggressive, angular lugs, deeper and more pronounced than anything she typically encountered. It suggested a vehicle with serious off-road capability, or perhaps a more utilitarian purpose. They were not the tracks of a casual joyride. They spoke of intent, of a vehicle brought here for a specific, perhaps clandestine, reason. Esme traced the outline of one of the impressions with her finger, feeling the subtle ridges. The width was also notable; it suggested a wider tire than average, hinting at a larger vehicle, a truck perhaps, or a powerful SUV.

She followed the faint trail with her eyes as it veered off towards the less-trafficked perimeter of the park, disappearing into a patch of overgrown brush near the old oak tree. It was a direction that suggested a deliberate attempt to avoid the main thoroughfares, a move calculated to minimize the chances of being seen.

Esme made a mental note of the general direction, the way the tracks veered towards the less-traveled edge of town.

Her skates were invaluable here. They allowed her to cover ground quickly, to pivot and reposition herself for different angles without the cumbersome effort of walking. She circled back to the starting point, then skated along the edge of the pathway, her eyes meticulously searching the verge. The dew was starting to burn off as the sun began its slow ascent, and she knew her window for finding such subtle clues was closing.

It was then, near the base of the old oak, where the tire tracks seemed to vanish into the thicker undergrowth, that she spotted something else. A small, dark smudge on a patch of exposed soil. It wasn't a leaf, nor was it a clump of mud. It was too uniform, too distinct. Esme approached cautiously, her heart giving a little leap of excitement. She knelt again, bringing her face closer.

The smudge was roughly circular, about the size of a quarter, and appeared to be some kind of greasy residue. It had a slightly iridescent sheen in the nascent sunlight, suggesting it might be oil-based, or perhaps a specialized lubricant. It wasn't the kind of everyday grime you'd find in a park. She carefully extended a small, sterile plastic evidence bag she'd brought with her, the kind used for collecting small samples. With the tip of a clean twig, she nudged the smudge into the bag, sealing it with a gentle press.

This was tangible. This was *something*. It wasn't just a feeling or a overheard snippet of conversation; it was a physical trace left behind. The tire tracks spoke of a vehicle's presence, and this smudge, however small, might speak of the *nature* of that presence, or even the cargo it carried. Was it from the vehicle itself? Or perhaps from the individuals who had tampered with Rex?

Esme stood up, her mind racing, piecing together these nascent fragments of evidence. The aggressive tire tracks, leading away from the scene into less visible areas, combined with the peculiar residue. It painted a picture that was far more organized than a spontaneous act of vandalism. The conversations she'd overheard at the Sonic about 'unusual acquisitions' and a 'rendezvous' suddenly felt more grounded, more sinister.

She skated back towards the center of the park, her gaze sweeping across the wider area. She needed to confirm if these tracks were indeed isolated, or if there were other signs of unusual activity. She circled the entire perimeter of the park, her skates gliding silently over the pathways and the dew-laden grass. She found no further tire impressions of the same distinctive pattern, which suggested that the vehicle had likely made its approach and departure from a specific point, possibly the area near the oak tree, and had not simply driven through the park's main entrances.

The lack of other tracks was, in itself, informative. It indicated a degree of care, a deliberate effort to minimize their presence. They hadn't just driven anywhere; they'd targeted a specific spot and likely parked nearby, out of immediate sight. The brush near the oak tree was dense enough to conceal a vehicle, especially in the dim light of early morning or late evening.

Esme paused, leaning against the cool metal of the park fence. She closed her eyes for a moment, letting the information settle. The tire tracks were a physical link, a direct connection to the means of Rex's removal. The smudge was a potential identifier, a unique characteristic that might, with the right knowledge, lead back to a specific type of vehicle or even a particular owner.

This was the difference between speculation and investigation. The overheard words in the alleyway and the whispers in the diner had provided the narrative, the suspicion of something illicit. But these physical clues – the tire impressions and the residue – were the footnotes, the concrete evidence that grounded the narrative in reality. They provided a starting point for a more targeted inquiry, moving beyond vague suspicions to specific questions: what kind of vehicle leaves tracks like that? What is this smudge made of?

Her skates felt like an extension of her own senses, allowing her to experience the scene in a way that would be impossible on foot. She could glide, circle, and gain different perspectives with an effortless fluidity. She skated a wider arc around the oak tree, peering into the dense foliage, trying to imagine where a vehicle might have been parked. The ground here was softer, more yielding, and it was easy to see how tracks could be obscured by the undergrowth.

She thought about the other details that had felt out of place. The raven button, for instance. Could it be connected to the vehicle or the people who drove it? Ravens were scavengers, often associated with dark places, with the fringes of society. If the tire tracks belonged to a vehicle used for illicit purposes, perhaps the raven symbol was a subtle mark of their association. It was a leap, she knew, but in the absence of clear answers, every tangential piece of information deserved consideration.

Esme took out her phone, snapping a few clear pictures of the tire tracks, documenting their direction and their approximate location. She also took a close-up shot of the smudge within its bag, ensuring the lighting was adequate. She knew she couldn't analyze the residue herself, but she could show it to someone who might have the expertise, perhaps Mr. Henderson, who had an encyclopedic knowledge of all things mechanical and industrial in Rio Seco. Or maybe even Mrs. Gable, who, despite her quiet demeanor, was surprisingly well-connected through her volunteer work.

The thought of the upcoming Founder's Day parade lingered in her mind. Rex's absence would be keenly felt, a gaping hole in the heart of the celebration. The timing of the theft was too precise to be mere coincidence. It felt like a deliberate disruption, a statement of some kind, as one of the diner patrons had suggested. But what kind of statement? And why Rex?

Her skates were her mobility, her stealth, and her advantage. While others might be limited to walking the scene, Esme could cover more ground, examine more angles, and move with a speed and discretion that was invaluable. She was no longer just a delivery girl; she was a scout, a detective in the making, piecing together the scattered fragments of a crime that was becoming increasingly complex. The initial mystery of a missing town mascot was rapidly evolving into something far more intricate, hinting at a network of individuals with specific vehicles, hidden motives, and a plan that extended beyond the simple act of theft. The footprint of their operation, however faint, was starting to emerge.

The morning air, still thick with the scent of damp earth and blooming jasmine, held a fragile peace. Esme, however, knew that peace in Rio Seco was often as fleeting as the morning mist. The missing Rex, the enigmatic tire tracks, and the faint, greasy smudge were a potent cocktail of unease that had settled over her. She needed more than just physical clues; she needed eyes and ears that had witnessed the town when its guard was down, eyes that could see beyond the obvious. And for that, there was only one person in Rio Seco who fit the bill: Mr. Henderson.

Mr. Henderson was a fixture in Rio Seco, as much a part of the town's landscape as the old clock tower or the perpetually blooming bougainvillea that cascaded over the town hall. He was Rio Seco's resident grump, a man whose disposition seemed to bloom only when tending to his meticulously manicured roses. His garden, a riot of color and fragrance that bordered the town square, was legendary, a testament to his obsessive dedication. It was also, Esme suspected, the best vantage point in town for observing anything out of the ordinary, especially under the cloak of night. Henderson, with his early rising habits and his deep-seated distrust of anyone who dared to tread on his perfectly edged lawns, saw everything.

Navigating her skates towards his property was always a delicate operation. Mr. Henderson's gardens were not merely plants; they were a carefully curated, fiercely protected kingdom, and any intrusion was met with a verbal barrage that could wilt the hardiest petunia. Esme slowed her approach, her skates gliding with practiced grace over the worn cobblestones of the sidewalk that skirted his domain. She gave his prize-winning 'Crimson Glory' roses a wide berth, their velvety petals a deep, almost bruised red, their thorns a silent warning. She'd learned long ago that the most effective way to get anything from Mr. Henderson was to appear as unobtrusive as possible, a shadow passing by, a whisper in the wind.

As she neared the low stone wall that marked the outer boundary of his garden, she could see him. He was already there, a hunched figure in worn overalls, his face obscured by the wide brim of a straw hat, his hands, gnarled and earth-stained, moving with a practiced, almost surgical precision as he deadheaded a spent bloom. The air around him seemed to vibrate with an almost palpable irritation, as if the very act of photosynthesis was an inconvenience.

"Morning, Mr. Henderson," Esme called out, keeping her voice light and pleasant, the kind of voice that wouldn't startle a robin from its nest, let alone enrage a gardener guarding his petunias.

He didn't look up immediately. His movements continued, a rhythmic pruning that seemed to ignore her presence. The silence stretched, taut and expectant, punctuated only by the faint *snip* of his secateurs and the distant chirping of sparrows. Esme waited, her skates poised, ready to glide away if the omens were unfavorable.

Finally, with a sigh that sounded like a gust of wind through a dry cornfield, he straightened his back, his shoulders protesting the movement. He turned, his gaze, sharp and piercing as a hawk's, fixing on her. His eyes, watery and blue, seemed to hold a permanent disapproval, a lifetime's worth of judging weeds and wayward slugs.

"What do you want, girl?" His voice was a gravelly rumble, laced with the ingrained cantankerousness of a man who had spent eighty years communicating with plants, and found humans significantly more difficult. "Can't you see I'm busy? These aphids aren't going to eradicate themselves, you know. And you're disturbing the dewfall on my dahlias. Think, child, think before you skitter about like a startled rabbit."

Esme offered a placating smile. "Just passing by, Mr. Henderson. Saw you out early. Thought I'd say hello." She paused, then plunged ahead, deciding honesty, or at least a version of it, was the best approach. "Actually, I was hoping you might have seen something… unusual last night. Near the town square."

His bushy eyebrows, white and sparse, drew together in a frown. "Unusual? What's unusual in Rio Seco? A bird singing off-key? A cloud shaped like a misplaced watering can? This town runs on a predictable cycle of boredom, broken only by the occasional over-enthusiastic fireworks display." He gestured with his secateurs, narrowly missing a particularly vibrant fuchsia. "And don't tell me you're here about that ridiculous armadillo. Honestly, a town mascot made of fiberglass. What kind of self-respecting animal would allow itself to be stuffed and paraded around? It's an insult to nature."

Esme felt a flicker of annoyance, but she tamped it down. "Rex is important to the town, Mr. Henderson.

And he's missing. Vanished. From his pedestal right in the middle of the square."

He snorted, a sound remarkably like a pig being startled. "Vanished? More likely some hooligans took it for a joyride and dumped it in the old quarry. Serves the council right for investing taxpayer money in such a gaudy monstrosity. Anyway, what's that got to do with me? I'm a gardener, not a detective. My concerns are chlorophyll and compost, not misplaced plastic lizards."

"But you're always out here, Mr. Henderson," Esme pressed, her skates subtly shifting her position to maintain his attention. "You see everything that comes and goes. Especially at night. I was wondering if you saw any cars… any unusual vehicles parked near the square, late last night, or in the very early hours of this morning."

He paused, his gaze drifting towards the town square, a distant, unseeing stare that suggested he was accessing a different kind of memory, one not filled with pruning shears and pest control. He was silent for a long moment, his silence more telling than any outburst.

Esme held her breath, watching the subtle flicker of his eyelids.

Then, he cleared his throat, a dry, rasping sound. "Cars," he muttered, more to himself than to her. "Always cars. Always noise. Ruining the peace. Always parking where they shouldn't." He took a slow breath, as if savoring the memory, or perhaps just gathering the will to speak. "Last night, you say?"

Esme nodded eagerly, her skates almost vibrating with anticipation. "Yes. Sometime after midnight, perhaps. Or very early this morning."

He squinted, as if trying to focus on a faint impression. "There was… yes. There was one. Parked down by the old fountain. Not the usual ones, mind you. Not the farmer's trucks, or Mrs. Gable's sensible sedan, or those noisy little jalopies the youngsters drive. This was… different."

Esme leaned in slightly, her skates making a soft whirring sound against the paving stones. "Different how, Mr. Henderson?"

He scowled, as if the memory was an unpleasant weed he was being forced to uproot. "Sleek. Low to the ground. Dark colored. And the engine… when it finally started up, it didn't sound like any engine I've heard around here before. A deep thrum, almost a growl. Not like a farm tractor, or even one of those fancy sports cars that sometimes pass through on their way to the coast. This sounded… powerful. And quiet, too, until it was time to leave."

A sleek, low-slung car. A powerful, rumbling engine. It certainly didn't sound like the usual Rio Seco fare. Esme mentally compared this description to the tire tracks she'd found. Aggressive tread, wider than average. It fit.

"Where did it come from, Mr. Henderson? Did you see it arrive?"

He huffed. "Arrive? I don't keep track of every beetle that crawls into my garden, girl. I was out here at… what time was it? Before the baker starts his infernal racket. I was tending to my night-blooming cereus. Magnificent thing, you know. Opens only for a few hours, then it's gone. Requires absolute stillness. And that's when I noticed it. Parked there, silent as a tomb, under the old oak tree by the fountain. Not where anyone usually parks. Certainly not during the day, and barely at night."

He gestured with his secateurs towards the edge of the town square, his movements still jerky and impatient. "Right there. Close to the bushes. Not on the paved area, but just off it. Like it was trying to hide, but not very effectively. The lights were off. I couldn't see much, just the shape of it. But it was definitely out of place. It had an… air of purpose about it. Not a casual visitor's car."

"An air of purpose," Esme repeated, filing the phrase away. "And you're sure it was there before midnight? Or rather, that it left sometime after midnight?"

"I was out here, like I said, for the cereus. It bloomed. I watched it. Then, I went back inside. It was quiet then. Later, when I heard that engine… that's when I looked out the window again. And the car was gone. The space under the oak tree was empty, just as it should be." He gave a decisive nod, as if closing a particularly stubborn iris bloom. "It was gone. And so was that… that plastic armadillo, I suppose."

Esme felt a surge of adrenaline. This was it. The confirmation she needed. An outsider, with a distinctive vehicle, present at the scene of the crime during the crucial hours.

"Did you see anyone get out of the car, Mr. Henderson? Or get into it?"

He shook his head, his straw hat wobbling precariously. "No. Too dark. And I wasn't about to go poking my nose where it wasn't wanted. Besides, my cereus was the main event. A fleeting beauty. Cars are ephemeral nuisances." He sighed again, a sound of profound weariness. "You know, child, the problem with this town is that everyone thinks they know everyone else. They think they know what's going on. But they don't. They see what they expect to see. They don't see the things that creep in from the edges."

He squinted at Esme, his gaze suddenly shrewd. "You're not just asking because the town's lost its silly mascot, are you? You've got that look. The one that says you're digging for something more."

Esme met his gaze, a slight smile touching her lips. "Maybe I am, Mr. Henderson. Maybe I am."

He grunted, turning back to his roses. "Well, don't expect me to tell you anything else. My observations are my own. And my roses are my priority. Now, if you'll excuse me, these weeds are practically mocking me. And don't let me see you skating near those petunias again. They're particularly sensitive to vibrations."

Esme didn't need to be told twice. She gave him a polite nod, a silent thank you for the crucial piece of information. As she skated away, the image of the sleek, dark car and its powerful, rumbling engine was seared into her mind. Mr. Henderson, the grumpy gardener, had just provided the first concrete lead that pointed away from local mischief and towards something more organized, more deliberate, and undoubtedly more sinister. The trail was getting warmer, and Esme felt a thrill of anticipation mixed with a healthy dose of apprehension. The wheels of investigation were finally starting to turn, propelled by the grudging observations of a man who preferred the company of flowers to people, but who, in his own curmudgeonly way, had seen enough to illuminate the shadows. The mystery of Rex's disappearance was no longer just about a missing mascot; it was about a carefully planned operation, and the arrival of unwelcome, unknown elements into the peaceful rhythm of Rio Seco.

The confirmation from Mr. Henderson had ignited a new spark in Esme. The image of the sleek, dark car with its guttural growl had shifted her focus from the predictable, sun-drenched heart of Rio Seco to its periphery. The town square, with its familiar fountain and the empty pedestal where Rex once stood, now felt like a stage set for a play that had already ended. The real action, the true clues, lay beyond the manicured lawns and the gossiping housewives. They lay in the forgotten corners, the places Rio Seco preferred to ignore.

Her skates, usually a tool for navigating familiar routes, now felt like instruments of exploration. The cobblestones of the main street soon gave way to rougher terrain. The smooth, predictable glide was replaced by a more cautious, deliberate dance over cracked asphalt and then, jarringly, onto a dirt track that wound away from the town's heart. This was the edge of Esme's known world, the boundary where Rio Seco's carefully cultivated tranquility began to fray.

The first stretch was still recognizable, a road that led towards the old cannery, a relic of the town's industrial past, now standing as a hollowed-out shell. Its brickwork, once a symbol of prosperity, was now stained with neglect, its windows shattered like vacant eyes staring out at the encroaching scrubland. Esme steered her skates onto the uneven ground beside the road, the jarring vibrations traveling up her legs. The scent of jasmine and damp earth was replaced by the musty odor of decay and forgotten machinery. This was not a place for casual strolls; it was a place whispered about in hushed tones, a place where stories of trespassers and strange occurrences festered.

She continued onward, the late morning sun casting long, distorted shadows that seemed to reach out like grasping fingers. The track narrowed, becoming less of a road and more of a suggestion, a faint scar on the landscape. The silence here was different from the quietude of the town square. It was a heavy, expectant silence, punctuated only by the rasp of dry grass against her wheels and the distant caw of a crow.

Her mind replayed Mr. Henderson's description: "Sleek. Low to the ground. Dark colored. And the engine… a deep thrum, almost a growl. Powerful. And quiet, too, until it was time to leave." She imagined the car navigating this very track, its suspension groaning under the strain, its dark paint a stark contrast against the dusty earth. Had it come this way? Or had it arrived via another forgotten path, another artery leading into the town's less-traveled arteries?

She reached a fork in the track. One path veered towards a cluster of abandoned farmhouses, their roofs sagging, their fences broken, looking like skeletal remains of a once-thriving agricultural community. The other path plunged into a denser thicket of mesquite and prickly pear, seemingly leading nowhere. Mr.

Henderson had mentioned parking near the old fountain, close to the bushes. That suggested an entrance or exit point not directly onto the main square but from its periphery, from a place where one could easily slip in and out unseen.

Esme chose the path leading towards the farmhouses. They were the kind of places that held their secrets close, stories of families who had packed up and left, leaving behind only echoes and dust. As she skated closer, the wind whistled through the gaps in the rotting wood, creating a mournful symphony. She scanned the ground, her eyes sharp, searching for any anomaly. Tire tracks, disturbed earth, anything that spoke of recent passage.

She found it near the largest farmhouse, the one with a faded blue door still hanging precariously on its hinges. Not the distinct aggressive tread she'd found by the fountain, but a different pattern, fainter, as if the vehicle had been moving slowly, cautiously. It was a single, partial imprint, partially obscured by fallen leaves and dried mud. It was wider than a standard car tire, but the tread pattern was less aggressive than the one that had been imprinted in the damp earth near the town square. This suggested a potential change in vehicle, or perhaps a different approach to this less-traveled area. Had the car that took Rex been swapped? Or had it simply used different tires for different terrains? The possibilities multiplied, each one pulling her further into the maze.

She spent an hour exploring the vicinity of the abandoned farmhouses. She circled each structure, her skates a silent whisper against the dry, cracked earth. She peered into darkened windows, imagining the lives that had once filled these spaces, and felt a pang of sympathy for the forgotten stories. But there was no immediate sign of Rex, no obvious trail leading from this desolate spot. The mystery remained stubbornly opaque, its tendrils reaching into these forgotten corners.

Frustrated but not defeated, Esme turned her attention to the other path, the one that disappeared into the dense scrubland. This was truly the wilderness, the parts of Rio Seco that even the most seasoned locals avoided. The vegetation grew thick and tangled, a thorny embrace that seemed to push back against any intrusion. The sun, now higher in the sky, was fierce, beating down on her exposed skin.

She had to dismount her skates, tucking them under her arm, and proceed on foot, pushing through the thorny branches, her jeans snagging and tearing. The air was thick with the scent of dry earth and wild herbs. She kept a sharp eye on the ground, her senses heightened. This felt like venturing into the unknown, a true "skating the periphery" in every sense of the word.

The terrain was uneven, littered with loose rocks and hidden roots. She stumbled several times, her hands instinctively reaching out to brace herself against the unforgiving landscape. She was well and truly out of her comfort zone now, the familiar order of the town replaced by the chaotic, untamed beauty of the natural world. But within this wildness, she felt a strange sense of freedom, a detachment from the expectations and limitations of her everyday life.

After what felt like miles of pushing through the undergrowth, she emerged into a small, unexpected clearing. In the center of the clearing stood an old, rusted water tower, its metal groaning in the wind. It was a solitary sentinel, a monument to a forgotten purpose. And there, near its base, half-hidden by overgrown weeds, was something that made her heart leap.

It was a patch of disturbed earth, much fresher than the faint imprints she'd found at the farmhouses. And in the center of this patch, partially covered by a thin layer of dust, was a distinct imprint of a tire. This one was different from the one by the fountain. It was wider, with a more aggressive tread pattern, a series of deep, angular grooves that spoke of excellent traction, of a vehicle designed to grip and hold. It matched the description of the tracks she'd found near the town square.

Her breath hitched. This was it. This was the connection. The sleek, dark car with the powerful engine had been here, in this secluded clearing, away from prying eyes. But why? Was this a meeting point? A place to transfer Rex? Or was this just a detour, a brief stop on a larger journey?

She knelt, carefully examining the ground. There were other signs too: faint scuff marks, as if something heavy had been dragged, and a few snapped twigs on a nearby mesquite bush, at a height that suggested a person moving with purpose, perhaps carrying something. She ran her fingers over the tire imprint, the rough texture of the rubber imprinted in her memory. It was a tangible link, a piece of the puzzle that had been missing.

As she stood up, surveying the clearing, her gaze fell upon a faint, almost imperceptible trail leading away from the water tower, disappearing back into the dense vegetation. It was not a well-worn path, but a series of subtle disturbances in the undergrowth, suggesting a deliberate, if discreet, passage. It was a route that avoided the main tracks, a hidden artery within the wild.

A thrill of discovery coursed through her. The investigation was no longer confined to the tidy streets of Rio Seco. It had taken her to the edge, to the forgotten places, and now, it was leading her even further, into the heart of the wilderness. She imagined the dark car, its powerful engine a low growl, navigating this hidden trail, its destination unknown.

She carefully noted the location of the tire imprint, marking it mentally. She knew she couldn't linger. The sun was beginning its descent, and the journey back would take time. But she had found a crucial piece of evidence, a confirmation that the missing Rex hadn't simply been a local prank. This was something else entirely, something that involved a vehicle capable of traversing rough terrain, a vehicle that had been operating in secrecy.

As she retraced her steps, her mind raced. Where did this hidden trail lead? What was the purpose of this secluded clearing? And most importantly, where had the car, and Rex, gone from here? The periphery of Rio Seco was revealing its secrets, but each revelation only opened up a wider vista of unknowns. She was no longer just skating the periphery; she was charting it, mapping its hidden contours, and with each discovery, the mystery deepened, pulling her further into its enigmatic embrace. The silence of the wilderness now seemed to hold a thousand whispered questions, and Esme was determined to find their answers, no matter how far off the beaten path they led. The path back to town felt different now, no longer a familiar route, but a passage through territory that had suddenly become charged with unspoken dangers and tantalizing possibilities. The periphery was not just a location; it was a state of mind, and Esme was rapidly embracing it.

3: Encounters and Entanglements

The dust from the neglected track swirled around Esme's skates as she ventured further from the familiar, sun-drenched center of Rio Seco. The air, once alive with the scent of jasmine and the distant murmur of the town, now carried the dry, earthy perfume of scrubland and the faint, metallic tang of sun-baked earth. She was on a self-assigned patrol, a mission fueled by Mr. Henderson's unsettling description of the sleek, dark car and its guttural engine – a stark contrast to the placid serenity Rio Seco so carefully cultivated. The abandoned cannery, a skeletal monument to a bygone era, had been her first stop, its shattered windows like vacant eyes staring into the encroaching wilderness. From there, a barely-there track had beckoned, a faint scar on the landscape leading towards the skeletal remains of forgotten farmhouses. She'd found a partial tire imprint there, fainter than the aggressive tread she'd discovered near the town square, suggesting a possible vehicle change or a different approach to these less-traveled arteries.

Her path now led her away from the ghost towns of agriculture and deeper into the wilder fringes, a territory that even the most adventurous locals tended to give a wide berth. The scrub thickened, thorny branches snagging at her jeans as she pushed through, eventually forcing her to dismount her skates, tucking them under her arm. The sun beat down with an insistent intensity, the silence broken only by the rasp of dry leaves and the distant, mournful cry of a hawk circling overhead. It was in this untamed expanse, where the edges of Rio Seco dissolved into a rugged, indifferent landscape, that she found herself at a dusty crossroads. Not a formal intersection marked by signs or pavement, but a natural convergence of several faint trails, a place where the earth itself seemed to hesitate before deciding which direction to surrender.

And there, leaning against the gnarled, ancient trunk of an old oak tree, was a figure.

Esme froze, her breath catching in her throat. The individual was silhouetted against the bright, harsh light, making it difficult to discern their features clearly, but their presence was undeniable, a solitary island in the sea of scrub. They were not engaged in any obvious activity – no picnicking, no birdwatching, no leisurely stroll. They were simply… there. Leaning. Waiting? Watching? The posture was relaxed, almost casual, yet an immediate prickle of unease traced its way up Esme's spine. This was not a place where people typically lingered. It was a junction of forgotten paths, a place of transition, not destination.

She instinctively ducked behind a thick clump of prickly pear cactus, its formidable spines a natural, if uncomfortable, shield. Her skates, still tucked under her arm, felt heavier, a potential burden rather than a tool of swift escape in this uneven terrain. From her concealed vantage point, she squinted, trying to pierce the glare and the distance. The figure was dressed in muted colors, blending into the dry, dusty landscape, making them even harder to identify. They were lean, their stance suggesting a certain coiled energy, as if they could spring into motion at any moment. They were turned slightly away from her, their gaze fixed on one of the diverging trails, their head tilted as if listening.

This stranger's presence felt deliberate, a stark anomaly in the predictable rhythm of her investigation. Rio Seco was a town where everyone knew everyone, or at least, everyone knew *of* everyone. This was someone she didn't recognize, someone who didn't belong to the familiar tapestry of the town. Their furtive demeanor, the way they seemed to be observing the trails rather than simply enjoying the solitude of the wilderness, ignited her suspicions. Was this person connected to Rex's disappearance? Had they seen something? Or were they, perhaps, involved?

Her mind immediately flashed back to Mr. Henderson's words. "Sleek. Dark. Powerful." She tried to superimpose the image of the car onto the solitary figure. It was a futile exercise, of course. This was a human being, not a machine. But the instinct to connect every new piece of information, every unknown variable, to the central mystery was strong. This person was an unknown variable.

She remained still for a long moment, her senses on high alert. The silence of the wilderness pressed in, amplified by the heightened awareness of her own heartbeat thrumming in her ears. The figure shifted, their head turning slowly, their gaze sweeping across the landscape. For a heart-stopping second, Esme thought their eyes might land on her hiding spot. She held her breath, pressing herself further into the scratchy embrace of the cactus. But their gaze moved on, unseeing, or perhaps deliberately overlooking.

Slowly, cautiously, Esme began to edge her way around the clump of cactus, moving from shadow to shadow, using the sparse vegetation as cover. Her goal was to gain a better vantage point, to try and catch a clearer glimpse of the stranger's face, their build, anything that might offer a clue. Her skates made little noise on the dry earth, but she was acutely aware of every rustle, every dislodged pebble.

As she rounded a particularly dense mesquite bush, the stranger turned more fully, and Esme finally saw their profile. It was a young man, or perhaps a very young man. His hair was dark, cut short, and he wore a plain, dark t-shirt and jeans. There was a subtle tension in his shoulders, a wariness in the way he scanned his surroundings. He looked… watchful. And there was something in his eyes, even from this distance, that spoke of an awareness beyond the ordinary. He wasn't just enjoying the scenery; he was guarding something, or waiting for someone.

He reached into his pocket, and Esme tensed, expecting him to pull out a phone, a weapon, anything that might confirm her suspicions. Instead, he produced a small, worn leather-bound notebook and a pencil. He opened the notebook, his brow furrowed in concentration, and began to scribble something down. His movements were quick, efficient, almost practiced. He then looked up again, his gaze still fixed on the trail ahead, his posture unchanged.

The notebook. That was a new element. What was he documenting? The arrival of someone? The passing of a vehicle? Or was he keeping a log of his own observations? Esme filed the detail away, her mind already weaving it into the growing tapestry of the mystery.

She knew she couldn't stay hidden forever. The sun was climbing higher, and the heat was becoming more oppressive. Moreover, if this stranger was indeed connected to Rex's disappearance, engaging with him directly, even from a distance, carried its own risks. Her skates, now gripped tightly in her hands, offered a clear advantage. If she needed to make a hasty retreat, she could be on them and moving within seconds, faster than anyone on foot in this rough terrain.

She decided to try a different approach. Instead of trying to circle closer, she moved back a little, angling herself towards the trail the stranger seemed to be watching. She would pretend to be an explorer, someone who had stumbled upon this crossroads by accident, and see how he reacted. It was a calculated risk, but the potential for information outweighed the danger.

She emerged from behind the mesquite bush, her skates now on her feet, her movements deliberately casual. She skated onto the dusty path, making a show of looking around with mild curiosity, as if she had just arrived at this junction herself. She made sure her skates made a soft, rhythmic sound, announcing her presence without being aggressive.

The stranger's head snapped up at the sound. His body tensed, his hand instinctively going to his hip. He watched her approach, his gaze sharp and assessing. Esme offered a small, friendly smile, trying to project an aura of harmlessness.

"Hello," she called out, her voice deliberately pitched to sound cheerful and a little surprised. "Didn't expect to see anyone else out this far."

The stranger didn't immediately respond. He continued to watch her, his expression unreadable. He slowly straightened up from his leaning position, his movements fluid and economical. He was taller than she had initially thought, and his frame was wiry, suggesting strength rather than bulk.

"Just… passing through," he replied, his voice low and somewhat raspy, as if he didn't use it often. His eyes, now that she could see them more clearly, were a dark, intense shade of brown, and they held a disconcerting stillness. They seemed to take in everything, processing details with an unnerving efficiency.

Esme skated a little closer, stopping about twenty feet away from him. The distance felt safe, yet close enough to observe his reactions. "Me too," she said, gesturing vaguely down the path she had come from. "Exploring the… wilder parts of Rio Seco. It's quite beautiful, isn't it? In a rugged sort of way."

He didn't return the smile. His gaze flickered from her face to her skates, then back to her face. There was a subtle appraisal in his look, a silent question. "Some find beauty in it," he conceded, his tone noncommittal. He then turned his attention back to the trail he had been watching, as if her presence was an interruption, albeit one he was prepared to tolerate.

This was not the open, friendly exchange she had hoped for. His reticence, his guardedness, only deepened her suspicion. He wasn't just passing through; he was here for a reason, and he clearly wasn't interested in sharing it.

"Do you live around here?" Esme pressed, trying another angle. "I don't think I've seen you around town."

He finally looked at her fully again, and for a brief moment, a flicker of something – amusement? Annoyance? – crossed his features before it was gone, replaced by the same impassive mask. "No," he said curtly. "Just visiting."

"Oh, really?" Esme feigned a bright interest. "For how long?"

He shrugged, a small, almost imperceptible movement. "Hard to say." He then shifted his weight, his gaze drifting back to the trail. It was a clear dismissal, a signal that the conversation was over.

Esme felt a surge of frustration. He was being deliberately evasive, a classic sign of someone with something to hide. But she also recognized the futility of pushing too hard. He was not going to give her any information willingly.

She decided to take one last gamble, a calculated risk that might either confirm her suspicions or expose her own investigation. "It's funny, you know," she said, her voice casual, as if recalling a minor detail. "I've been looking for a particular car. Dark, sleek, low to the ground. Heard its engine sometimes. Quite distinctive." She watched him closely, searching for any telltale reaction.

His body stiffened almost imperceptibly. His eyes narrowed slightly, and his hand, which had been resting casually on his hip, tightened its grip. It was a small reaction, almost undetectable, but Esme caught it. He knew what she was talking about.

"Haven't seen anything like that," he said, his voice still carefully neutral, but with a new, subtle edge to it. "This isn't exactly a main road, you know. People tend to keep to themselves out here."

"Oh, I know," Esme agreed, nodding slowly, her mind racing. His reaction was confirmation enough. He was connected to the car. And if he was connected to the car, he was likely connected to Rex's disappearance. "But I was hoping someone might have seen something. It's important."

He gave a short, humorless laugh. "Everything's important to someone," he said, his gaze now fixed on her skates. "Especially when you're out here looking for things."

His words hung in the air, a veiled warning. He knew she was investigating. He knew she was looking for something. And he clearly didn't appreciate her presence.

Esme knew it was time to go. She had gathered enough information, and staying any longer would be foolish. She gave him another small, deliberately unconcerned smile. "Well, thanks for the chat," she said brightly. "Enjoy your… visit."

Without waiting for a response, she turned her skates and skated away, heading down the main path, the one that led back towards the more populated areas of Rio Seco. She didn't look back, but she could feel his gaze on her, a tangible weight on her back. The silence that followed her departure was heavy with unspoken implications.

As she skated further away, the encounter replayed itself in her mind. The stranger's watchful eyes, his terse responses, the subtle tension in his posture, the casual mention of the notebook – it all painted a picture of someone involved in clandestine activities. He was not an innocent bystander. He was a piece of the puzzle, a significant one.

She reached a bend in the path that obscured the crossroads from view. Only then did she allow herself to slow down, her heart still pounding with adrenaline. The encounter had been brief, but it had yielded crucial information. The stranger's reaction to her mention of the car was undeniable. He was connected. The mystery was no longer confined to the whispers and rumors of Rio Seco; it had taken on a tangible, human form, a silent watcher at the edge of town, guarding his secrets at a forgotten crossroads. The wild parts of Rio Seco were not just beautiful; they were also dangerous, and Esme had just encountered one of its inhabitants, a guardian of secrets, standing sentinel at the intersection of the known and the unknown. The path ahead still held its mysteries, but now, Esme felt a renewed sense of purpose, armed with the unsettling knowledge that she was not alone in her search, and that the shadows of Rio Seco held more than just forgotten memories.

The stranger's terse dismissal echoed in Esme's mind as she continued to skate, the rhythmic crunch of her wheels on the dusty track a stark counterpoint to the sudden silence that had fallen over the crossroads. She hadn't gone far, just far enough to put a reasonable distance between herself and the enigmatic figure, before veering off the main path and finding a secluded spot behind a cluster of sun-bleached boulders. From this vantage point, she could still see the solitary figure, though he was now partially obscured by a low-hanging mesquite. He hadn't moved from his spot by the oak tree, his silhouette a dark, still punctuation mark against the shimmering heat haze. He was still looking down the trail, his attention seemingly unwavering. Esme pulled her skates off, her movements quick and practiced, and tucked them under her arm once more. The silence here was deeper, more profound, broken only by the faint buzz of insects and the rustle of unseen creatures in the undergrowth.

She waited, her senses on high alert, the earlier encounter playing over and over in her mind. His guardedness, his curt responses, and especially that almost imperceptible stiffening when she'd mentioned the car – it all pointed to something far removed from a casual desert excursion. He was a piece of the puzzle, a dark, silent piece that had just revealed a sliver of its significance. She wondered if he was waiting for someone, or for something, to emerge from the very trail he was so intently watching. The thought sent a shiver down her spine, despite the oppressive heat.

Then, he moved. Not towards her, nor towards the trail he'd been scrutinizing, but back in the direction of the main track she had just departed. He walked with a deliberate, unhurried gait, his hands behind his back, his head bowed slightly. Esme stayed hidden, her breath held, watching him approach the crossroads. He paused there for a moment, his gaze sweeping across the landscape in a way that suggested he was checking for any lingering signs of her presence. Apparently satisfied, he turned and began to move along the main track, heading away from her, back towards the direction of Rio Seco, but on a different fork than the one she'd taken.

As he moved further away, Esme noticed something else. Not far from the oak tree where he had been standing, almost hidden in the shadow of its thick trunk, was a small, weathered payphone booth. It looked impossibly old, a relic from a bygone era, its metal casing peeling and rusted, its glass panels clouded with dust. Esme blinked, surprised. Payphones were a rarity, almost an anachronism, in Rio Seco. Most people relied on cell phones, and even those were spotty in these more remote areas. This booth, however, looked like it hadn't seen a working coin in years.

Yet, as she watched, the stranger approached it. He reached out, his fingers brushing against the grimy surface of the booth, as if testing its sturdiness. Then, to her utter astonishment, he pulled a coin from his pocket – a silver dollar, glinting in the harsh sunlight – and inserted it into the slot. The coin clinked, a surprisingly loud sound in the stillness, and the dial tone buzzed to life.

Esme strained her ears, her heart hammering against her ribs. He was making a call. And she was close enough, with the wind carrying sounds across the open ground, to potentially overhear something. She crept forward, inch by agonizing inch, positioning herself behind a large, thorny bush that offered a decent screen, her skates clutched tightly. The stranger turned his back to her as he spoke into the receiver, his voice low and muffled by the confines of the booth.

"Yeah, it's me," he began, his voice the same raspy, low tone she'd heard earlier. "Look, we've got a problem."

Esme's breath hitched. A problem. This was it. The confirmation she'd been seeking.

"No, nothing went as planned," he continued, his voice dropping even lower, becoming almost a whisper. He paused, listening to the response on the other end. "The whole damn thing. It's off. We're pulling out."

Pulling out? Off? Esme's mind raced. This was clearly not a casual conversation about a fishing trip or a delayed delivery. This was coded language, or perhaps just blunt, straightforward talk about a failed operation. The 'deal' was off. He was 'laying low'.

"No, I told you, it's off," he repeated, a hint of impatience creeping into his voice. "The drop point was compromised. Or maybe… maybe it was never viable to begin with. The intel was bad. Whatever it is, the arrangement is nullified."

The drop point. Compromised. Esme's mind immediately flashed to Rex, to the missing mascot, to the strange tire tracks. Was this 'drop point' related to where Rex had disappeared? Was the 'deal' somehow connected to the disappearance? The questions tumbled over each other in her mind, each one more urgent than the last.

He listened for another moment, his brow furrowed. "I don't know. I can't say. The directive was clear: if anything felt off, we abort. And things feel very off." He rubbed his temple with his free hand, a gesture of clear frustration. "Yeah, I'll lay low. Find a place. And I'll be in touch when it's safe. Don't try to contact me unless it's an absolute emergency. Understood?"

He listened again, a curt nod serving as his final acknowledgement. "Alright. Later."

He hung up the receiver, the click of the hook sounding unnervingly final. He stood there for a moment, his shoulders slumped slightly, before pocketing the coin and turning away from the booth. He glanced back at the oak tree, then in the direction of the crossroads, his eyes sweeping the area with that same unnerving vigilance. Esme pressed herself flatter against the ground, praying she hadn't been seen.

He didn't linger. He walked with a purpose now, heading off the main track and disappearing into the denser scrub, the same direction he had initially gone. Esme waited until the sound of his footsteps had completely faded, until the only sounds were the persistent hum of insects and the faint whisper of the wind.

Slowly, cautiously, she rose to her feet. The payphone booth loomed before her, a silent witness to the clandestine conversation. She peered into it, her fingers tracing the worn metal of the handset. The air inside still seemed to hold the echo of his hushed, urgent words. 'Nothing went as planned… the deal is off… need to lay low.'

This was far beyond a simple missing mascot. This was something darker, something more dangerous. The stranger was not just a curious wanderer; he was involved in something that had gone wrong, something that required him to 'lay low'. The missing mascot, the strange car – these were no longer isolated incidents. They were threads in a much larger, and potentially more sinister, tapestry.

She looked in the direction the stranger had gone, a knot of unease tightening in her stomach. He had said he would 'lay low'. Where would someone like him go to disappear in a place like Rio Seco? He was a stranger, unburdened by local ties, able to blend into the anonymity of the vast, empty landscape.

Her gaze fell back on the payphone. It was a tool of connection, a way to communicate when other methods were too risky. But it was also a signifier of a certain kind of operation, one that relied on discreet communication, on meeting points and clandestine arrangements.

Esme returned to her skates, her mind a whirlwind of new possibilities and escalating concerns. The initial investigation into the missing mascot had suddenly taken a sharp, precipitous turn. The stranger, with his guarded demeanor and his urgent phone call, had just confirmed that the mystery was far more complex and dangerous than she had initially imagined. He was a key piece of the puzzle, a direct link to whatever had caused 'the deal' to go off.

She knew she couldn't simply dismiss this. The faint tire tracks, the sleek dark car, the overheard conversation – they all pointed to a confluence of events that were deeply unsettling. The wild parts of Rio Seco, once merely the backdrop to her exploration, now felt like a labyrinth of secrets, populated by individuals with hidden agendas and dangerous connections. The stranger's words, "lay low," now seemed to apply not just to him, but to the entire unsettling situation. And Esme, with her skates and her insatiable curiosity, found herself deeper in the tangle than ever before. She had stumbled upon a conversation that confirmed her deepest suspicions and simultaneously opened up a terrifying new vista of unanswered questions. The simplicity of a missing school mascot had dissolved, replaced by the chilling intimation of something far more significant, something that had gone terribly wrong in the desolate heart of Rio Seco. The whisper of "the deal is off" was now a roar in her ears, a siren call to a deeper, more perilous investigation.

The echo of the stranger's hushed, urgent words continued to resonate in Esme's mind, a persistent undercurrent beneath the mundane rhythm of her life. The phrase "lay low" felt like a personal directive, a constant reminder of the unseen currents swirling beneath the surface of Rio Seco. But laying low was a luxury she couldn't afford. Her world, once a predictable cycle of school, work, and the occasional skate, had been irrevocably complicated. The meticulously crafted schedule that had once governed her days now felt like a fragile façade, strained by the weight of secrets and the gnawing need for answers.

Her shifts at Sonic, once a simple means to earn money for skating gear and the occasional indulgence, now served a dual purpose. Each customer interaction, each order taken, was a potential opportunity to glean some fragment of information, however insignificant. She found herself listening more intently to the chatter between customers, her ears perked for any mention of unusual activity, unfamiliar faces, or anything that might remotely connect to the sleek, dark car or the man she'd overheard at the payphone. It was a tiring, often fruitless endeavor. Most conversations were the usual small-town gossip, talk of the upcoming football game, complaints about the heat, or discussions about the dwindling water supply. Still, she persisted, her mind a finely tuned instrument, constantly sifting through the noise for a signal.

The challenge of maintaining this dual existence was immense. Lectures that had once held her attention now felt like distant echoes. While Professor Davies droned on about the socio-economic impact of irrigation in arid regions, Esme's gaze would drift, her thoughts snagged by the memory of the stranger's curt tone or the glint of the silver dollar. She'd find herself mentally replaying the overheard conversation, dissecting each word, each pause, searching for hidden meanings. Sometimes, she'd pull out her notebook, ostensibly to jot down lecture notes, but in reality, she'd be sketching crude diagrams of crossroads, or writing down snippets of overheard phrases, trying to piece together the fragmented narrative. This mental gymnastics often left her feeling exhausted, a thin layer of fatigue clinging to her like the desert dust.

The transition from school to work was a blur. The moment the final bell rang, a surge of adrenaline would propel her. The twenty-minute walk to Sonic felt like an eternity, and she'd often find herself breaking into a run, her backpack bouncing against her shoulders, her skates still tucked away, waiting for their moment. She'd arrive at her Sonic uniform, pulling on the familiar red shirt and visor, a silent apology to her body for the exertion, before plastering on a cheerful smile. "Welcome to Sonic, what can I get for you?" The words felt rote, a performance she was increasingly adept at.

Between taking orders, mixing milkshakes, and delivering food to carhops, her mind would still be miles away, back at that desolate crossroads. She'd catch herself staring out the window, her eyes scanning the passing cars, half-expecting to see that elusive dark sedan. The desert landscape surrounding Rio Seco, once a familiar and comforting expanse, now felt like a vast, watchful entity, capable of harboring secrets and concealing dangers. Every dust devil that swirled across the highway, every distant plume of dust from an unseen vehicle, sent a jolt of nervous energy through her.

Her parents, thankfully, remained oblivious to the full extent of her extracurricular activities. They knew about the skating, of course, and the part-time job at

Sonic. But the clandestine investigation, the whispers of a compromised deal, and the unsettling encounter with a mysterious stranger were safely hidden behind her carefully constructed normalcy. She'd come home, feign tiredness from her 'long' day, and retreat to her room, the door a thin barrier between her carefully curated reality and the increasingly complex truth.

The stolen moments she managed to snatch for herself were dedicated to further investigation. Late at night, after her parents had gone to bed, she'd pore over local maps, tracing the roads she'd skated, trying to pinpoint potential "drop points" or areas that might offer secluded spots for clandestine meetings. She'd also spent hours online, researching coded language, survivalist tactics, and even, in her more paranoid moments, the types of organizations that might operate in such a discreet manner. The internet, a gateway to a world far removed from Rio Seco's sleepy streets, became her digital sanctuary, a place where she could pursue answers without raising suspicion.

One particularly challenging afternoon, after a double shift at Sonic and a particularly draining history lecture where she'd nearly fallen asleep, Esme found herself staring blankly at a math problem. The numbers swam before her eyes, utterly meaningless. Her mind was fixated on the tire tracks she'd noticed near the oak tree. They had been distinct, almost too perfect, and she couldn't shake the feeling that they were significant. Were they from the stranger's car? Or were they from someone else entirely, someone connected to whatever had gone wrong? The thought sent a shiver down her spine.

She sighed, pushing the textbook away. This wasn't sustainable. Trying to be a diligent student, a reliable Sonic employee, and a burgeoning detective all at once was taking its toll. She felt stretched thin, her focus fractured. The thrill of discovery, which had initially fueled her, was now tempered by a growing sense of weariness and a gnawing anxiety. The desert, which had always represented freedom and escape, now felt like a cage, trapping her in a web of unanswered questions.

Later that week, during her shift, Mrs. Gable, a regular at Sonic who was known for her sharp tongue and even sharper eyesight, came through the drive-thru. As Esme handed over her usual order of a strawberry shake and fries, Mrs. Gable leaned out her car window, her voice barely a whisper. "Saw a funny-looking car out by the old county road yesterday, Esme. Dark, fancy. Not the kind of thing you usually see out there. Looked like it was parked for a while, then just… vanished."

Esme's heart leaped. "Oh yeah?" she managed, her voice carefully neutral. "Did you see who was in it?"

Mrs. Gable pursed her lips. "Couldn't tell. Too far away. But it struck me as odd. Out in the middle of nowhere like that."

The encounter, however brief, was a small victory. It was another confirmation, another piece of the puzzle clicking into place. The stranger's car, the dark, sleek vehicle Mrs. Gable had seen – they were almost certainly connected. The fact that it was parked for a while, then vanished, mirrored the stranger's own sudden appearance and disappearance.

The weight of these discoveries pressed down on her. She was no longer just a curious teenager looking into a missing mascot. She had stumbled into something far more complex, something that involved clandestine phone calls, "deals" going off, and unidentified vehicles lurking in the desolate corners of Rio Seco. The simple act of balancing her life had become an intricate dance, a precarious tightrope walk between the mundane demands of adolescence and the dangerous allure of a truth that refused to stay buried. Every moment of normalcy was a carefully managed performance, a shell around the burgeoning reality of her secret investigation. She knew, with a certainty that both thrilled and terrified her, that this balancing act was only just beginning. The path ahead was uncertain, fraught with potential peril, but the pull of the mystery, the insistent whisper of the unanswered questions, was too strong to ignore. She would continue to skate, to work, to study, all while weaving her way through the shadows, searching for the truth that lay hidden beneath the vast, indifferent sky of Rio Seco.

The afternoon sun, usually a benevolent presence in Rio Seco, felt more like a relentless interrogation lamp as Esme pushed herself through the familiar dusty streets. Her skates hummed against the worn asphalt, each rotation a beat in the increasingly complex rhythm of her thoughts. The echo of Mrs. Gable's observation, coupled with the lingering unease from the payphone encounter, had coalesced into a new direction for her burgeoning investigation. It was a long shot, a shot fueled more by desperation and a hunch than any concrete evidence, but it was a direction nonetheless.

She steered her skates towards a part of town she rarely ventured into, a cluster of older buildings that seemed to cling to their faded glory. Nestled between a shuttered hardware store and a laundromat perpetually shrouded in steam, was her destination: 'Curiosities and Oddities.' The shop's name was painted in peeling gold leaf on a dark, weathered sign that hung precariously from a single chain. It was a place whispered about more than visited, a repository of forgotten stories and the strange detritus of lives long past.

The shop itself was a testament to its name. The windows were crammed with an eclectic, almost chaotic, assortment of items: a chipped porcelain doll with one vacant eye staring out, a tarnished silver tea set, a collection of hats that seemed to brim with unspoken histories, and a taxidermied owl perched regally on a stack of leather-bound books. Even from the street, a faint, sweetish scent of dust, old paper, and something indefinably metallic hung in the air. It was the kind of place where you half-expected a hidden door to swing open, revealing a secret passage or a portal to another time.

Taking a deep breath, Esme nudged the shop's door with her shoulder. A tiny bell, perched precariously on a spring above the doorframe, let out a muffled, discordant jingle. The interior was even more densely packed than the windows suggested. Every surface was covered, every corner occupied. Narrow aisles snaked between towering stacks of furniture draped in dust sheets, shelves overflowing with trinkets, ceramics, and more books. The air inside was thick and still, the sunlight filtering through the grimy windows casting ethereal shafts of light that illuminated dancing motes of dust. It felt less like a shop and more like a carefully curated hoard, each object imbued with its own silent narrative.

Presiding over this kingdom of the peculiar was a man who seemed to have been assembled from the shop's own collection. Mr. Abernathy was a study in eccentricities. He was tall and gaunt, with a shock of unruly white hair that defied gravity and a pair of wire-rimmed spectacles perched precariously on the end of his long, thin nose. He wore a waistcoat that was several decades out of fashion, embroidered with faded floral patterns, over a crisp, though slightly rumpled, white shirt. His movements were deliberate, almost languid, as he carefully polished a brass sextant with a soft cloth.

He looked up as the bell announced Esme's arrival, his eyes, magnified by his glasses, seeming to take in her entire being in a single, unhurried glance. There was an immediate impression of intense, almost unsettling, perception. He didn't simply see; he observed, cataloged, and perhaps, Esme suspected, understood far more than he let on.

"Well, well," Mr. Abernathy said, his voice a low, reedy baritone that seemed to vibrate with the accumulated dust of ages. "A new face in the sanctuary of the forgotten. To what do I owe the pleasure, young lady? Seeking a relic to anchor your memories, perhaps?"

Esme felt a flicker of self-consciousness. She hadn't really prepared a story, relying on her usual ability to improvise. "Just… browsing, Mr. Abernathy," she replied, her voice a little softer than she intended. "I heard you have some… interesting things here."

A slow smile spread across Mr. Abernathy's thin lips, crinkling the corners of his eyes. "Interesting," he mused, testing the word as if it were a rare spice. "Indeed. Interesting is merely a stepping stone to the truly fascinating, and from there, to the utterly peculiar. What particular brand of 'interesting' brings you to my humble establishment today?" He gestured vaguely with the polishing cloth, encompassing the entirety of the shop's cluttered embrace.

Esme took another tentative step inside, the floorboards creaking a protest. She kept her eyes scanning the shelves, trying to appear casual, while her mind raced to formulate her question. She couldn't just ask about a specific car. That would be too direct, too suspicious. She needed to approach it indirectly, to plant the seed and see if he would water it.

"I'm interested in… unusual vehicles," she began, choosing her words carefully. "Like, cars or perhaps even… trailers, that might not belong here. Things that stand out." She tried to inject a note of casual curiosity into her voice, as if she were simply indulging a passing whim.

Mr. Abernathy paused in his polishing, his gaze sharpening. He lowered the sextant and stepped from behind his counter, moving with surprising agility for someone who looked so frail. He walked slowly towards a glass display case filled with antique pocket watches, his head tilted as if listening to a distant conversation.

"Unusual vehicles, you say?" he repeated, his voice taking on a more thoughtful, almost dramatic, cadence. "Rio Seco, for all its placid charms, can sometimes attract the… transient. The vehicles that pass through are often as much a part of the story as the people who drive them. Tell me, what sort of 'unusual' are we discussing? A flamboyant chariot for a circus performer? A sturdy workhorse for a prospector of forgotten dreams?"

Esme's heart gave a nervous little flutter. He was playing along, but there was a glint in his eye that suggested he was more than just indulging her. He was intrigued. "More like… something out of place," she offered. "Something sleek, maybe dark. Something that looks… important, but also a bit out of its element here." She hesitated, then added, "I've seen a few things recently that just… didn't fit."

Mr. Abernathy stopped in front of the display case, his fingers tracing the intricate patterns on a silver fob. He didn't look at her directly, but his stillness was more telling than any movement. The silence stretched, punctuated only by the distant hum of traffic and the faint ticking of unseen clocks. Esme held her breath, waiting for his response. She felt as though she were navigating a minefield, each word a potential misstep.

Finally, he turned back to her, a small, enigmatic smile playing on his lips. "Ah, yes. The 'out of place' vehicles. They often leave ripples, don't they? Like a stone cast into a still pond. And sometimes," he leaned in slightly, his voice dropping to a conspiratorial whisper, "they come with… particular requests."

This was it. The opening she'd been looking for. "Requests?" Esme prompted, her gaze locked on his.

Mr. Abernathy picked up another polishing cloth, this one a vibrant emerald green. He began to meticulously clean the glass of the display case, as if the very act of cleaning could reveal hidden truths. "Indeed. A gentleman, a week or so ago. Distinguished, well-dressed, but with a certain… urgency about him. He wasn't interested in pocket watches or snuff boxes. His focus was elsewhere." He tapped a long, bony finger against the glass, directly in front of a particularly ornate birdcage.

Esme's eyes followed his gesture. The birdcage was exquisite. Crafted from what looked like polished brass, it was a miniature aviary of intricate filigree, with tiny doors and a delicate perch. It was far too elaborate to be a common item, and it certainly looked like something that belonged in a different era, or a different place entirely. But it was the detail that caught her breath. She remembered seeing something remarkably similar.

"He purchased something rather specific," Mr. Abernathy continued, oblivious to Esme's sudden internal alarm bells. "He was looking for a rather particular vessel. Something that could contain… flight, perhaps? Or at least the illusion of it." He gestured towards the birdcage. "This little beauty. Solid brass,

rather charming, wouldn't you say? He paid handsomely for it."

Esme's mind flashed back to the day of the mascot's disappearance. She'd been skating along the edge of the woods, not far from the crossroads where she'd later overheard the hushed conversation. She'd seen the dark sedan parked on the shoulder, partially concealed by overgrown brush. And near it, glinting in the dappled sunlight, had been something metallic. She hadn't paid it much mind at the time, thinking it was just a discarded piece of equipment, but now… now it clicked into place with a sickening certainty.

"A birdcage?" Esme asked, her voice barely a whisper. "What would someone want with a birdcage like that?"

Mr. Abernathy shrugged, his gaze returning to the sextant he'd been polishing earlier. "Ah, that is the perennial question, isn't it? The purpose. The intent. Most items that find their way here have a past, a story. This gentleman, however, seemed more concerned with the future. He spoke of… transporting something precious. Something that needed a secure, yet perhaps visible, enclosure." He paused, then added, with a theatrical flourish, "He mentioned it needed to be sturdy, but also capable of allowing one to observe its… occupant."

Esme felt a chill creep up her spine. 'Transporting something precious.' 'Observe its occupant.' It sounded so innocuous, but coupled with the context of the overheard conversation, of a "deal" that had gone wrong, of a missing item, it painted a far more sinister picture. The mascot hadn't simply been misplaced; it had been taken. And this elaborate birdcage, this 'vessel for flight,' was somehow connected.

"Did he… did he say where he was going?" Esme pressed, trying to keep her tone light, as if she were merely curious about the provenance of the item.

Mr. Abernathy chuckled, a dry, rustling sound. "My dear girl, if I possessed such information, my establishment would likely be a museum of state secrets rather than a purveyor of forgotten curiosities. He was quite discreet. Paid in cash, left no name. A ghost with excellent taste in brassware." He tilted his head, his eyes now fixed on Esme with an unnerving intensity. "You seem remarkably interested in this particular piece. It's not often that young ladies of your… energetic disposition take such a keen interest in antique avian accommodations."

Esme felt her cheeks flush. She knew she was being too obvious, too eager. But the tangible link, the physical object that connected the mysterious stranger and his overheard words to a specific location and a specific transaction, was too significant to ignore. It was the first concrete clue she'd found, something more substantial than a fleeting glimpse of a car or a snippet of conversation.

"It's just… very beautiful," she said, trying to recover. "I've never seen anything like it. I love old things." She gestured vaguely around the shop. "I guess I appreciate things that have a history."

Mr. Abernathy's gaze softened almost imperceptibly. He seemed to understand her unspoken distress, her search for something more than just historical appreciation. "Indeed," he said, his voice losing its theatrical edge and settling into something more genuine. "Everything here has a history, young lady. Some louder than others. Some whisper secrets, some shout warnings. This birdcage," he gestured to it again, "speaks of captivity, perhaps. Or of a gilded freedom. It's a matter of perspective, wouldn't you agree?"

Esme nodded, her mind already racing. If this birdcage was indeed connected, then the person who bought it was someone she needed to find. And if that person was connected to the dark sedan, and the hushed conversation, then she might be getting closer to understanding what had happened to the missing mascot. She needed more information about this "gentleman," about his plans, about where he might have taken the birdcage.

"Do you remember anything else about him?" Esme asked, pushing her luck. "Anything at all? What he looked like, perhaps? Or where he might have come from?"

Mr. Abernathy's eyes twinkled behind his spectacles. He picked up the brass sextant again, turning it over and over in his hands. "He had the scent of expensive cologne, the kind that clings to the air long after the wearer has departed. And his hands… his hands were remarkably clean. Pristine, even. Not the hands of someone who works with their hands, but someone who… directs them. And perhaps," he paused, "he had a faint accent. Not strong, but discernible. Something… eastern, perhaps?"

An accent. Clean hands. Expensive cologne. It was a fragmented picture, but it was more than she'd had before. She thanked Mr. Abernathy, promising to return soon, and slipped back out into the blinding sunlight, the jingle of the bell a poignant farewell. The birdcage, a symbol of both exquisite craftsmanship and hidden purpose, was seared into her memory.

As she skated away from 'Curiosities and Oddities,' the pieces of the puzzle began to shift, rearranging themselves into a more coherent, and terrifying, pattern. The dark sedan, the hushed conversation, the missing mascot, and now, the ornate birdcage bought by a well-dressed stranger with an elusive accent. It was all starting to coalesce, pointing towards something far more deliberate and organized than she had initially imagined. Rio Seco, the sleepy desert town she thought she knew, was proving to be a stage for secrets she was only just beginning to uncover. The birdcage, with its implied containment, was a chilling reminder that whatever was being transported was likely not meant to be seen by the general public. And Esme knew, with a certainty that settled deep in her gut, that her investigation had just taken a far more dangerous turn. She wasn't just looking for a missing mascot anymore; she was chasing a shadow, a shadow that dealt in exquisite brass cages and carried the scent of expensive secrets.

The scent of old paper and dust, still clinging to Esme's clothes from Mr. Abernathy's shop, seemed to amplify the oppressive heat of the Rio Seco afternoon. Her skates felt heavy, each rotation a deliberate, almost weary, push against the familiar resistance of the cracked pavement. The information gleaned from the antique dealer had been a jolt, a tangible thread connecting the whispers and shadows to something concrete, yet it had also plunged her deeper into an unsettling realization: this wasn't just about a missing mascot anymore. The elegant birdcage, purchased by a man with a subtle accent and meticulously clean hands, hinted at a far more calculated operation, one that

whispered of clandestine exchanges and concealed movements.

She found herself drawn to the quieter side of town, the residential streets where the houses, though weathered, still held a sense of settled history. It was a stark contrast to the dusty, transient aura that seemed to surround the recent events. She was on her way to the library, a place she usually associated with quiet afternoons and overdue notices, but today it felt like a potential haven, a place where information, even if buried deep within the Dewey Decimal System, might be found. It was a long shot, but after Mr. Abernathy's cryptic revelations, she was willing to try anything.

The Rio Seco Public Library was a modest, unassuming building, constructed from the same sun-baked adobe that characterized many of the older structures in town. A cool, dim interior greeted her, a welcome respite from the glare outside. The air inside was thick with the comforting scent of aging paper, binding glue, and the faint, sweetish aroma of floor polish. A handful of patrons were scattered throughout the reading rooms, their hushed movements and the rustle of turning pages creating a symphony of quiet industry.

Behind the circulation desk, a figure was meticulously sorting returned books, their movements precise and almost methodical. It was Elias Vance, the town's quiet archivist and unofficial historian. Elias was a familiar presence in Rio Seco, a man of quiet habits and an almost encyclopedic knowledge of the town's past. He was a lanky man, with perpetually ink-stained fingers and a perpetually thoughtful expression, his sharp blue eyes often hidden behind thick-rimmed glasses that seemed to magnify his gaze. He was the kind of person who noticed things, who absorbed the subtle shifts in the town's rhythm, the quiet arrivals and departures that most people overlooked.

Esme approached the desk, the distinctive hum of her skates a sudden, intrusive sound in the hushed sanctuary. Elias looked up, a flicker of recognition in his eyes, followed by a subtle nod. He didn't offer a customary greeting, but his posture shifted, a subtle readiness that Esme, now attuned to the nuances of people's reactions, registered immediately.

"Mr. Vance," Esme began, her voice softer than usual, a conscious effort to match the library's hushed atmosphere. "I was hoping you might be able to help me. I'm looking for some old town records… specifically, information about local businesses, maybe even… car registries from a few years back."

Elias set down the book he was holding, his hands coming to rest on the polished oak of the counter. His gaze, usually directed at the pages before him, now met Esme's directly, and there was something in his eyes that went beyond polite inquiry. It was a look of keen observation, of understanding, and perhaps, she dared to hope, of shared curiosity.

"Old records, you say?" Elias's voice was a low murmur, barely disturbing the quiet. "The library's collection is extensive, though some of the older archives can be… temperamental to access. What exactly are you hoping to find?"

Esme hesitated. She couldn't simply blurt out her suspicions about the dark sedan or the mysterious birdcage. But Elias Vance was different. He was a quiet observer, a keeper of secrets, and there was a stillness about him that suggested he might be more than he appeared. She decided to risk a partial truth, a carefully worded breadcrumb.

"I'm trying to trace the movements of certain vehicles," she explained, choosing her words with care. "Some cars that might have passed through Rio Seco, perhaps not for long. I'm interested in anything that might have seemed… out of the ordinary. Unusual business dealings, maybe, or vehicles that weren't registered locally."

Elias leaned back slightly, his fingers tapping a silent rhythm on the counter. He seemed to be mulling over her request, his gaze drifting to a dusty framed map of Rio Seco hanging on the wall behind her. "Out of the ordinary," he echoed, his voice thoughtful. "Rio Seco has a way of attracting those who wish to remain… unobserved. They often leave faint trails, if one knows where to look."

Esme felt a prickle of anticipation. He understood. He wasn't just a librarian; he was a seeker of patterns, a curator of the overlooked. "You've seen them too, haven't you?" she blurted out, the words escaping before she could properly censor them. "The cars that don't belong. The people who seem to be here for a reason, and then… they're gone."

Elias's expression didn't change, but a subtle tension entered his shoulders. He met her gaze again, and this time, there was a distinct acknowledgment in his eyes. He knew she wasn't just a curious teenager. He saw the earnestness, the determination that had fueled her day.

"I've observed many things, Esme," he said, his voice a little lower now, more intimate. "The comings and goings, the hushed conversations, the subtle shifts in the town's usual tempo. Rio Seco is a small town, and change, when it arrives, is often unmistakable. And recently," he paused, his eyes flicking towards the window, as if seeking confirmation from the bright desert sky, "there have been… deviations from the usual pattern."

Esme felt a surge of relief, a quiet sense of not being alone in her burgeoning unease. "I saw a dark sedan," she ventured, her voice barely above a whisper. "Parked near the old quarry road a few days ago. It looked out of place. And I… I overheard something.

About a 'deal' that went wrong, and something that needed to be moved quickly."

Elias's knuckles were white where he gripped the counter. He lowered his voice further, leaning in slightly. "A dark sedan," he repeated, his blue eyes sharp and focused. "I recall seeing one myself. Not near the quarry, but closer to the town's periphery, near the old airstrip. It was dusk, and the light was poor, but the vehicle was sleek, expensive. And the occupants… they were not locals."

Esme's breath hitched. The old airstrip. That was another place she hadn't considered, a relic of Rio Seco's more prosperous past, now mostly derelict and forgotten. "Did you see… what they were carrying?" she asked, her voice tight with a mixture of dread and anticipation.

Elias's gaze became distant, as if replaying a memory. "It was difficult to see clearly," he admitted. "They were loading something into the trunk. A long, rectangular object, I believe. Covered, perhaps. It was heavy, judging by the way they handled it. And the man who was overseeing the operation… he was dressed impeccably, as if he had just stepped out of a fashion magazine. He exuded an aura of authority, and a distinct air of impatience."

A long, rectangular object. Covered. Heavy. Esme's mind immediately went back to the birdcage, to the notion of a 'vessel for flight,' a secure enclosure. Could that be what they were loading? Was the mascot, or whatever it represented, the 'precious cargo' Mr. Abernathy had alluded to?

"Did you get a look at the man?" Esme pressed, her own thoughts racing ahead. "His face? Or anything distinctive about him?"

Elias shook his head slowly. "The light was failing, and he kept his back to me for the most part. However," he paused, a flicker of something, perhaps recognition, crossing his face, "he was wearing a distinctive signet ring on his left hand. Gold, with an intricate crest. It glinted in the dying light. And he had a particular way of speaking, even from that distance. A refined accent, quite unlike the rougher cadence of many of the transient workers we sometimes see."

The signet ring. The refined accent. It echoed Mr. Abernathy's description of the man who had bought the birdcage. The pieces were starting to fit together, forming a mosaic of a carefully orchestrated operation, one that involved people who were not from Rio Seco, people who operated with a certain sophistication and a need for discretion.

"I saw a similar man," Esme confessed, her voice hushed. "He bought something… unusual… from Mr. Abernathy's shop. Something that was meant to contain something. He had an accent, too. And his hands were very clean."

Elias's eyes widened slightly, a rare display of emotion from the usually stoic archivist. He understood the implication of her words. The 'unusual item' from Abernathy's, the 'long, rectangular object' at the airstrip, the man with the signet ring and the refined accent – they were all connected. He looked at Esme, a new respect dawning in his gaze. She wasn't just a kid chasing a lost item; she was piecing together a much larger, and potentially dangerous, puzzle.

"Mr. Abernathy's," Elias murmured, a slow smile spreading across his lips. "Of course. He deals in the curious, the forgotten. It makes sense that such a man would seek out his particular brand of 'storage.' He has a keen eye for those who operate in the shadows." He paused, then leaned forward again, his voice dropping to a conspiratorial tone. "I've been noticing a pattern myself, Esme. A series of anonymous donations to the historical society, always accompanied by cryptic notes. They seem to reference specific historical events, almost as if someone is trying to… document or perhaps even correct the historical record. The donations are always made through intermediaries, never directly."

Esme's mind reeled. Anonymous donations, cryptic notes, intermediaries… It sounded like a covert attempt to disseminate information, or perhaps to obscure it. Could these donations be connected to the mascot's disappearance? Was someone trying to cover their tracks, or leave a trail for someone to find?

"And the mascot," Esme added, the words a desperate plea for confirmation. "It wasn't just stolen, was it? Not randomly. It's connected to all of this, isn't it?"

Elias's gaze was steady, his expression serious. "The mascot is a symbol, Esme. A representation of something valuable, something of historical or perhaps even symbolic importance. Its disappearance is unlikely to be a mere act of vandalism. It's a deliberate removal, part of a larger purpose. And the man you described, the one with the signet ring, he fits the profile of someone orchestrating such an endeavor. Someone who operates with precision, with resources, and with a clear objective."

He then reached into a drawer beneath the counter and pulled out a small, leather-bound journal. He opened it carefully, revealing pages filled with meticulous handwriting and small, precise sketches. "I keep my own observations," he explained, his voice barely audible. "Of unusual vehicles, of unfamiliar faces, of conversations overheard. I noticed the dark sedan at the airstrip a few days ago, and then… I saw it again yesterday, parked near the old train depot. It seemed to be waiting."

Esme leaned closer, her eyes scanning the journal. Elias's notes were astonishingly detailed. He had documented license plate numbers, descriptions of people, even snippets of overheard dialogue. He had seen the dark sedan, the same one she had spotted near the quarry, now parked near the train depot, a place that had its own history of secret comings and goings.

"The train depot," Esme breathed, a new location, another piece of the puzzle falling into place. "Why there?"

"The old depot was once a hub of activity," Elias explained, his finger tracing a line on a faded map within the journal. "It still has access to unused tracks, discreet loading areas. It's a place where things can arrive and depart without attracting much attention." He looked directly at Esme, his blue eyes intense. "I believe our masked friends are preparing to move whatever they have acquired. And if your description of the birdcage is accurate, then the mascot, or whatever it represents, is likely already contained."

A profound understanding settled between them. They were both on the same path, albeit approaching it from different angles. Elias, with his meticulous record-keeping and quiet observation, and Esme, with her direct approach and skating-shoe-powered intuition. They recognized in each other a shared commitment to uncovering the truth, a silent acknowledgment that Rio Seco held secrets far more complex than it appeared.

"I want to help," Esme stated, her voice firm. "I have skates. I can move fast. I can try and see if that sedan is still there, or who else might be involved."

Elias considered her for a long moment, his gaze assessing her resolve. "It's dangerous, Esme. This is not a game of lost property. The people involved are… professional. They operate with a level of organization that suggests a significant operation."

"I know," Esme replied, meeting his gaze without flinching. "But I can't just stand by. I saw the mascot taken. I heard the conversations. And now… now I know it's more than just a mascot. It's something they're hiding. And I need to find out what."

A faint smile touched Elias's lips. It was a smile of genuine appreciation, of shared purpose. "You have a remarkable tenacity, Esme. It's a quality I admire." He closed the journal, his expression turning serious again. "I have managed to cross-reference some of the vehicle descriptions with old shipping manifests. There's a company, a… logistics firm, that has been mentioned in a few of the more obscure records. They specialize in discreet transport, high-value items. The name itself is… vague. 'Apex Logistics.'"

Apex Logistics. The name resonated with a cold, efficient promise. Esme pictured a sleek, unmarked truck, an anonymous warehouse. "Do you have any more information on them?"

"Only that their registered address is a post office box in a neighboring state," Elias admitted. "But I did find something else. A peculiar mention in an old local newspaper, from about five years ago. It detailed a… controversial exhibition at the town's historical society at the time, focusing on early Rio Seco artifacts. The exhibition was abruptly closed down due to a dispute over provenance and… missing items." He tapped his journal. "One of the items mentioned as having been part of that exhibition, and subsequently lost, was a beautifully crafted metal orb, inlaid with intricate patterns. It was described as 'unique' and 'of considerable historical significance.' And it was apparently housed in a very specific, custom-made cage."

Esme's blood ran cold. A metal orb, inlaid with intricate patterns, housed in a custom-made cage. It sounded eerily similar to the mascot's description, and the birdcage Mr. Abernathy had sold. The connection was becoming undeniable. This wasn't a random theft; it was a retrieval, an operation to reclaim something that had been taken years ago, something that had been part of a controversial exhibition. The mascot, she realized, was not just a mascot; it was a key, a symbol, a placeholder for something far more significant.

"The mascot wasn't just lost," Esme whispered, the realization dawning with full force. "It was stolen years ago, as part of that exhibition. And these people… they're trying to get it back. Or they think it's a legitimate claim."

"Or they are trying to sell it," Elias countered, his voice grim. "The 'dispute over provenance' could simply be a cover for theft. And if Apex Logistics is involved, then this is a professional operation with deep pockets. They are likely highly organized and well-equipped."

He looked at Esme, a new urgency in his gaze. "We need to be careful, Esme. We are two people trying to uncover something very large and very well hidden. I can provide you with historical context, potential leads, and a safe place to strategize. But you, with your mobility and your… fearlessness, you are the one who can gather the immediate intelligence. The sedan, the people, their movements."

A tentative alliance had formed, a shared secret forged in the hushed aisles of the library. Esme felt a weight lift, replaced by a surge of determination. She wasn't alone anymore. Elias Vance, the quiet archivist, was her unlikely ally, and together, they would uncover the truth behind the missing mascot and the shadowy dealings of Apex Logistics. The puzzle pieces were starting to click into place, revealing a picture far more intricate and perilous than she had ever imagined. The birdcage, the sedan, the man with the signet ring, the lost exhibition – it was all part of a story that had been unfolding in the shadows of Rio Seco for years, a story she was now irrevocably a part of.

4: The Trail Heats Up

The late afternoon sun beat down on the asphalt, the heat radiating upwards in visible waves, as Esme guided her skates back towards the quiet, unassuming street where she had first seen the ornate birdcage. The dusty air, still thick with the scent of sun-baked earth and mesquite, seemed to hum with a nervous energy, mirroring the thrumming in her own chest. She had left the library with Elias Vance, her mind buzzing with the implications of their conversation, the pieces of the puzzle slotting into place with a chilling precision. The birdcage, once an object of curious beauty purchased by a man with "meticulously clean hands" and a "subtle accent," now represented something far more sinister: a bespoke container, a vessel designed for transit, perhaps for the very mascot that had vanished from its pedestal.

She stopped near the curb, the familiar click of her skates the only sound breaking the oppressive stillness. The spot where the man had loaded the cage into the trunk of his sleek, dark sedan was still visible, a faint disturbance in the settled dust. Esme hopped off her skates, setting them down carefully, and knelt, running her fingers over the rough surface of the street. There, almost imperceptible, were faint scuff marks, linear and parallel, consistent with the dragging of something heavy, something being maneuvered into place. It wasn't the scrape of a dropped toolbox or the accidental drag of a suitcase. This was deliberate, controlled force. The shape of the marks suggested the base of something substantial, perhaps the sturdy, decorative stand that might have accompanied such an elaborate cage.

Her mind conjured the image Elias had painted: the impeccably dressed man with the signet ring, overseeing the loading of a "long, rectangular object, covered." Was that object the mascot itself, nestled within the confines of the very birdcage she had witnessed being purchased? The thought sent a shiver down her spine, despite the oppressive heat. Mr. Abernathy's cryptic words about the cage being "perfect for a special little treasure" now carried a heavy, loaded meaning. It wasn't a treasure of monetary value he was referring to, but something of historical significance, something that required discreet handling.

Esme stood, scanning the street. The houses here were quiet, their windows shuttered against the sun, giving them a watchful, almost indifferent air. No one seemed to have noticed anything out of the ordinary that day. The man with the birdcage had been meticulous, efficient. He had arrived, conducted his transaction, and departed with a silent haste, leaving behind only the faintest of traces for Elias and herself to discover. It was a testament to his professionalism, his need for anonymity. But anonymity, Esme knew, could also leave patterns, if one knew where to look.

Her skates were her advantage, her secret weapon in this quiet town. While others relied on cars that needed parking, on walking that took time, Esme could glide, a silent observer weaving through the backstreets and less-trafficked thoroughfares. She could cover ground quickly, revisit locations, and disappear as swiftly as she arrived. The library had been a wealth of information, Elias a vital ally, but now it was time for her to return to the physical landscape of the mystery.

She skated slowly down the block, her eyes catching on small details. A discarded cigarette butt near the curb – what brand? Did Elias mention anything about the occupants' habits? No, he'd been too far away to discern such specifics. A faint oil stain on the asphalt near where the sedan had been parked, slightly darker than the usual road grime. It was from the car, she was sure of it. Nothing more, nothing less. The city's heat seemed to press in, not just from the sun, but from the weight of the secrets it held.

She thought about Apex Logistics, the vague name Elias had unearthed. A company specializing in "discreet transport, high-value items." It sounded like the kind of outfit that moved art, or perhaps something more clandestine, something that couldn't be declared on a manifest. The connection to the controversial exhibition at the historical society five years ago, the missing metal orb housed in a custom cage – it was all starting to form a cohesive, albeit unsettling, narrative. The mascot wasn't just a mascot; it was the "metal orb," or rather, it was the *representation* of that orb, a physical link to an artifact that had been removed, likely stolen, from that exhibition. The current operation was a recovery, or perhaps a reselling, of something that had been taken years before.

The humid air felt thick, heavy with unspoken questions. Had the mascot been stolen as a bargaining chip? Was it being held for ransom? Or was its return to its rightful (or disputed) place the ultimate goal? The birdcage was the key, the meticulously crafted enclosure that allowed for the discreet transport of this valuable, contentious item.

Esme circled back towards the town center, her thoughts a whirlwind of possibilities. Elias had mentioned the old train depot. That was another location she needed to investigate. The depot, a place of departures and arrivals, of comings and goings that often went unnoticed, was the perfect staging ground for a clandestine transfer. If the sedan was still in town, it might be lurking near there, waiting for its next move.

Her skates felt like an extension of her own will, propelling her through the sun-drenched streets. The town, usually so familiar and comforting, now felt charged with a hidden current, a network of invisible threads connecting seemingly disparate events. The quiet streets, the dusty shops, the imposing façade of the library – they were all part of a larger stage upon which a complex drama was unfolding. And she, with her speed and her growing understanding, was a reluctant but determined player. The birdcage connection had solidified her purpose. It wasn't just about a missing mascot anymore; it was about unraveling a trail of deception that stretched back years, a trail marked by discreet transactions, hushed conversations, and objects moved in the shadows. The humid air of Rio Seco seemed to thicken with anticipation, as if the very atmosphere was holding its breath, waiting for the next move in this silent, unfolding game. She skated on, the rhythmic whir of her wheels a quiet counterpoint to the louder, more dangerous machinations that had been set in motion. The birdcage was the clue, the physical manifestation of a hidden purpose, and she was determined to follow where that purpose led, no matter how obscured the path. The sun began its slow descent, casting long shadows that seemed to deepen the mystery, and Esme, with a renewed sense of urgency, continued her silent vigil.

The humid air clung to Esme like a damp shroud as she skated back towards the intersection, the same one where she'd first spotted the stranger and his unusual cargo. The late afternoon sun, now beginning its descent, cast long, distorted shadows that danced and flickered across the asphalt, making the familiar streets feel alien and unnerving. Her mind replayed the snatched snippets of conversation, the cryptic phrases that had lodged themselves in her memory like burrs. "Nothing went as planned." The words echoed, a stark admission of failure, of deviation from an intended course. What plan? And what had gone awry? It suggested a meticulously laid scheme that had been disrupted, a carefully orchestrated operation that had, for reasons unknown, veered off its intended path.

"Lay low." That was the other phrase that gnawed at her. It wasn't just a suggestion; it was an imperative, a command born of a need for concealment, for invisibility. It spoke of a desire to disappear, to melt back into the anonymity from which they had emerged, at least until the immediate threat, whatever it was, had passed. Were they fugitives? Or simply individuals who operated in the shadows, accustomed to avoiding scrutiny? The urgency in the voice, even filtered through the ambient noise, had been palpable.

Esme's mind, a well-oiled machine for piecing together disparate clues, began to construct various scenarios. Who would hire someone to steal a mascot, especially one as unique and potentially valuable as the metal orb? The possibilities seemed to tumble out, each one more elaborate than the last. Perhaps it was a prank, a twisted adolescent dare gone too far. The late 1970s, with its burgeoning counter-culture and a general loosening of societal norms, was fertile ground for such outlandish schemes. Kids pulled elaborate stunts back then, driven by boredom and a desire to push boundaries. But the stranger's demeanor, the careful way he handled the ornate birdcage, the very specificity of its construction for a "special little treasure" – it all felt too calculated for a simple prank.

Or what if it was a collector? The metal orb, as Esme was increasingly convinced, was no mere mascot but a significant artifact, perhaps tied to the controversial exhibition five years prior. Collectors, especially those with an insatiable appetite for the unique and the historically significant, could be driven by a singular, all-consuming desire. They might commission the retrieval of items that had fallen into the wrong hands, or worse, items they believed were rightfully theirs. The "meticulously clean hands" and the "subtle accent"

Elias Vance had described painted a picture of someone precise, someone who likely operated in circles where such transactions were not unheard of.

But the phrase "nothing went as planned" hinted at more than just a failed acquisition. If a collector had hired them, it suggested they were expected to deliver the orb, intact and untainted. A botched retrieval implied complications, perhaps a botched handover, or even a misunderstanding about the nature of the item itself.

Then there was the possibility of something far more sinister, something that transcended mere acquisition or a childish prank. What if the orb, or the mascot it represented, was a key to something else? A piece of a larger puzzle, a catalyst for an event, or even a dangerous weapon. The late 70s weren't just about peace and love; they were also a time of burgeoning international intrigue, of Cold War tensions simmering beneath the surface, of clandestine operations and the illicit trade of secrets. Could this be something of that magnitude? Her gut, however, leaned away from such grand, global conspiracies. This felt… local. Rooted in the very soil of Rio Seco, albeit with an outsider's touch. The outsider's touch was crucial. The stranger, with his accent and his polished demeanor, didn't fit the familiar tapestry of the town. He was a foreign element, introduced into a local setting, and his presence, along with the botched plan, suggested a disruption of the local equilibrium.

Esme reached the intersection again, the asphalt still radiating the day's heat. She skated slowly, a silent sentinel, her eyes scanning the road, the sidewalks, the edges of the dusty lots. She was looking for any flicker of recognition, any anomaly that might have escaped her notice earlier. A different car, a lingering figure, a dropped item. Anything that could corroborate or contradict her nascent theories. The dust, stirred by the occasional passing car, swirled around her ankles, a constant reminder of the dryness and the stillness that often veiled deeper currents.

She recalled the birdcage's ornate details. Elias had described it as having intricate scrollwork, delicate filigree, and a small, almost insignificant lock. It wasn't just a cage; it was a statement. Designed to protect, yes, but also to display. Was the orb meant to be displayed, then? Or was the cage itself the prize, containing something hidden within its intricate bars? That seemed less likely, given the focus on the mascot's disappearance. The cage was a means, not an end.

The phrase "lay low" kept returning. It suggested they were aware of being watched, or at least of the potential for discovery. If their operation had indeed gone wrong, it was likely that whoever they were working for, or whoever they had stolen from, would be looking for them. And if they were being sought, they would naturally seek to evade detection. That meant staying out of sight, avoiding any actions that might draw attention. The stranger's disappearance into the labyrinthine backstreets of Rio Seco suddenly made more sense. He wasn't just driving away; he was actively seeking concealment.

She skated past the small diner where she had seen the stranger earlier that day. The windows were now darkened, the "Open" sign extinguished. It was a quiet place, unassuming, the kind of spot that wouldn't typically draw the attention of law enforcement or security. The perfect place for a clandestine meeting, or a brief respite. Had the conversation she'd overheard happened inside, or just outside, as she'd initially assumed? The acoustics of the street could be tricky. The sound of a passing truck could easily distort or mask voices.

She tried to visualize the stranger's face again, the brief glimpse she'd caught. He hadn't seemed overtly threatening, more… professional. Focused. The kind of person who takes pride in their work, whatever that work might be. But even the most professional individuals could be caught off guard, could make mistakes, could find their plans unraveling. The 'botched operation' narrative felt increasingly plausible.

What if the mascot *wasn't* stolen for a prank or for a collector, but rather for its intrinsic value, not monetary, but symbolic? The historical society's exhibition, the controversy surrounding the removal of the orb – these were key pieces. The orb, or its representation, had been removed once before. Perhaps this was a recovery effort, or a counter-effort. If the orb was indeed a stolen artifact, then this operation could be anything from a legitimate attempt to return it to its rightful place, to another illicit transfer, this time by someone with a different agenda.

The heat of the day was beginning to mellow, replaced by the softer glow of dusk. The shadows lengthened, merging into a velvety twilight. Esme continued her circuit, her skates a silent hum against the pavement. She was a detective of the overlooked, a cartographer of the forgotten corners of Rio Seco. The overheard conversation was her only tangible lead, a fragment of a larger, hidden narrative. And it was her job to reconstruct that narrative, one carefully considered possibility at a time. The stranger's motives remained a tantalizing enigma, a carefully guarded secret hidden behind a veneer of professionalism and a botched plan. But Esme was patient. She had time. And she had her skates.

The humid air, still thick with the day's stored warmth, began to cool as Esme skated towards the edge of town. The familiar hum of her wheels on the asphalt was a comforting counterpoint to the growing unease in her gut. The stranger, his cryptic words, and the vanished mascot – it all felt like a puzzle with too many missing pieces, and her mind, relentless as ever, was already sifting through potential connections. The thought of Oakhaven, that perpetually green, suspiciously chipper town just a few miles down the road, surfaced unbidden. Oakhaven. Their rivalry with Rio Seco was as old as the dusty main street they both shared, a simmering competition that intensified with every passing year, particularly as the annual County Fair loomed. And this year, Rio Seco's recently restored mascot, the gleaming metallic orb, was slated to be the star attraction, a symbol of their town's resurgent spirit after the ill-fated historical exhibit.

The idea took root, a tiny seed of a theory that began to sprout in the fertile ground of her speculation. Oakhaven. Their competitive nature wasn't just about winning ribbons at the fair; it was a deeply ingrained part of their town's identity, a constant, low-grade hum of one-upmanship directed squarely at Rio Seco. It was the kind of rivalry that festered, that bred grudges, and that sometimes, just sometimes, manifested in less than savory ways. Had the stranger, the one with the subtle accent and the peculiar cargo, been acting on behalf of Oakhaven? Or was there someone from Rio Seco itself, someone who had found their way to Oakhaven, who might harbor a desire to sabotage their town's moment of pride?

The drive, or rather, the skate, to Oakhaven was a familiar one. Esme knew the route by heart – past the old abandoned cannery, the cluster of whispering pines, and then the gradual incline that marked the transition from Rio Seco's sun-baked earth to Oakhaven's manicured lawns and meticulously maintained flowerbeds. Oakhaven always felt like a different world, a place where everything was just a little too perfect, a little too curated. Even their diner, 'The Oakhaven Omelet,' always seemed to have a shine on its windows that Rio Seco's 'Dottie's Diner' could only dream of.

She arrived as the sun dipped below the horizon, painting the sky in hues of orange and purple. The air here, too, carried the day's heat, but it was a different kind of heat, one tempered by the shade of abundant trees and the cool, damp scent of well-watered earth. Esme parked her skates near the town square, a pristine expanse of green dotted with blooming hydrangeas and a statue of some long-forgotten Oakhaven founder, looking resolutely at their own town with an air of smug satisfaction.

The Oakhaven Omelet was bustling, a symphony of clinking cutlery, murmured conversations, and the sizzle of bacon on the grill. Esme found a booth by the window, the kind that offered a good vantage point for people-watching and, more importantly, eavesdropping. She ordered a coffee, the dark, bitter liquid a welcome jolt to her system, and then she settled in, her senses on high alert, ready to catch any stray whispers, any dropped hints that might connect Oakhaven to the events back home.

She listened. She always listened. The conversations around her were a tapestry of Oakhaven life – complaints about the rising price of feed, discussions about the upcoming bake-off, excited chatter about the new county fair queen. But Esme wasn't looking for the mundane. She was searching for the discordant note, the hint of something out of place.

Then, she heard it. Two older women, their voices hushed but carrying easily in the diner's relative quiet, were talking about Rio Seco.

"Did you hear about Rio Seco's mascot?" one woman asked, her voice laced with a peculiar kind of glee. "The metal orb thing. They say it's gone missing, just before the fair."

The other woman chuckled, a dry, rustling sound. "Good riddance. Always thought it was a ghastly thing, that orb. And all that fuss over it, after… well, you know."

"Oh, I know," the first woman replied, her tone dropping conspiratorially. "But who would steal it? And why? Seems like a lot of trouble for a bit of old scrap metal."

"Perhaps it's not about the metal, dear," the second woman said, her eyes glinting. "Perhaps it's about… proving a point."

Esme's ears perked up. Proving a point. That sounded like something more than a simple prank. She strained to hear more, but the women lowered their voices even further, their conversation dissolving into an unintelligible murmur.

She scanned the diner again, her gaze sweeping across the faces. Most were familiar Oakhaven types — farmers, shopkeepers, the occasional retiree. But then her eyes landed on a man sitting alone at the counter, nursing a cup of coffee. He was younger, perhaps in his late twenties, with a certain rough-around-the-edges quality to him. His clothes were nondescript, his demeanor guarded. There was something about him that felt… off. He didn't quite fit the polished Oakhaven mold. He looked a bit like he belonged in Rio Seco, but with a harder edge.

He caught her looking, and his eyes, a pale, washed-out blue, flickered towards her for a moment before returning to his coffee. There was no warmth in his gaze, no curiosity, just a cool, dismissive assessment.

Esme decided to take a risk. She paid for her coffee and headed towards the counter, aiming to get a closer look. As she approached, she overheard a snippet of conversation between the man and the waitress.

"So, you're back in town for good, then, Danny?" the waitress asked, her tone friendly but also a little wary.

The man, Danny, grunted. "Suppose so. Nowhere else to go."

"Heard you were… out west for a spell," the waitress continued, her voice dropping slightly. "Business?"

Danny gave a short, humorless laugh. "Something like that. Learned a few things."

Danny. The name didn't ring a bell immediately, but the way he spoke, the slight gruffness that wasn't quite a Rio Seco drawl, made her wonder.

Esme moved to the seat next to him, her skates still on. The diner's floor, usually clean, had a faint sheen of grease near the counter. She sat down, deliberately making a slight scrape as she settled onto the stool.

Danny glanced at her, a flicker of annoyance in his eyes. He clearly wasn't interested in small talk.

"Rough day?" Esme ventured, feigning casualness.

He took a slow sip of his coffee. "What's it to you?" His voice was rough, unpolished.

"Just trying to make conversation," Esme replied, her smile unwavering. "It's a quiet Tuesday night."

"Not for everyone," he muttered, his gaze fixed on the condensation beading on his coffee cup.

Esme decided to push a little. "Heard some talk about Rio Seco's mascot going missing. Shame, that. Especially with the fair coming up."

Danny's head snapped up. His pale blue eyes met hers, and for a split second, there was a flash of something — surprise, perhaps, or maybe a guarded recognition. But it was gone as quickly as it appeared, replaced by his usual impassive expression.

"News travels fast," he said, his tone neutral, but Esme detected a subtle shift, a tightening of his jaw.

"It does," Esme agreed, leaning in slightly. "Especially when it's something as important as the Rio Seco orb. Big symbol for them, that is."

Danny shrugged, a deliberate, dismissive gesture. "Means nothing to me."

But his body language betrayed him. He'd tensed when she mentioned the orb, and now his knuckles were white where he gripped his coffee cup.

"You know, I heard some of the whispers," Esme continued, her voice a low murmur. "About why it might have been taken. Some people say it's a prank, a bit of bad blood between towns. Oakhaven, maybe?"

He gave another humorless laugh. "Oakhaven? They're too busy counting their prize-winning pumpkins to bother with Rio Seco's junk."

It was a denial, but it felt too quick, too dismissive. And the way he said "junk" — it was loaded, laced with a disdain that seemed to go beyond mere indifference.

"Funny," Esme mused aloud, her gaze fixed on his. "Because some folks in Oakhaven seem to think it's just the sort of thing *someone* might do. Someone who maybe felt… slighted by Rio Seco. Someone with a history of… let's call it 'petty mischief'."

Danny's eyes narrowed. He put his coffee cup down with a deliberate clink, the sound sharp in the sudden quiet of their immediate vicinity.

"And what would you know about my history?" he challenged, his voice dangerously low.

"I make it my business to know things," Esme said, her voice steady. She didn't know him, not really, but she recognized the type. The resentful, the overlooked, the ones who nursed grudges like precious heirlooms. And his presence in Oakhaven, his dismissive attitude towards Rio Seco, it all fit.

"You're from Rio Seco, aren't you?" Danny said, his gaze sharp and assessing. He seemed to be trying to place her, to figure out her angle.

"I am," Esme confirmed. "And I'm curious. Because Rio Seco might have its problems, but we also have our pride. And our mascot is part of that. And if someone's trying to undermine that, especially before the fair…" She let the sentence trail off, letting the implication hang in the air.

Danny leaned back, a slow, calculating smile spreading across his face. It wasn't a friendly smile. It was the smile of someone who knew something she didn't, or perhaps, someone who was enjoying her probing.

"You're asking the wrong questions, sweetheart," he said, his voice laced with a condescension that made Esme's jaw clench. "And you're in the wrong town."

He stood up, tossing a few crumpled bills onto the counter. "Oakhaven's got its own problems to worry about. Rio Seco's troubles are theirs alone."

He turned to leave, but Esme wasn't done. "Danny, right?" she called out.

He paused, his back to her. "What about it?"

"Danny… what's your last name?"

He hesitated for a fraction of a second, then turned his head slightly, his gaze lingering on her for a moment before he turned and walked out of the diner, disappearing into the Oakhaven night.

Esme watched him go, her mind racing. Danny. A former resident of Rio Seco, now apparently residing in Oakhaven. His bitterness, his dismissiveness, his possible connection to the missing mascot – it was all too much of a coincidence. He had the air of someone who felt wronged, someone who harbored a deep-seated resentment towards his former home. A grudge, fueled by whatever had driven him away from Rio Seco in the first place, could easily manifest as a desire to tarnish its newfound pride.

She lingered at the counter for a few more minutes, the waitress clearing away Danny's coffee cup.

"That Danny," the waitress said, shaking her head. "He's a strange one. Been back a few weeks now, keeps to himself. Used to live in Rio Seco, I heard. Left under… not the best circumstances, I think."

"Oh?" Esme prompted, her interest piqued.

"Yeah, something about a disagreement. Trouble with the town council, I think. Or maybe something with the historical society? Hard to say. He never really talked about it. Just came back here, looking like he'd lost his last dollar and found a nickel." The waitress gave a knowing nod. "He's got that look about him, the one that says he's carrying a chip on his shoulder the size of a boulder."

A chip the size of a boulder. That fit perfectly. A former Rio Seco resident, now living in Oakhaven, who had left under a cloud of controversy related to the town's history – perhaps even the very history that had led to the orb's controversial removal five years prior.

He would have had both the motive and, potentially, the local knowledge to orchestrate such a disappearance. His presence in Oakhaven, a town eager to see Rio Seco stumble, made him a prime suspect.

Esme thanked the waitress and slipped out of the diner, the night air cool against her skin. She found her skates and, with a practiced motion, began to glide back towards Rio Seco. The conversation in Oakhaven had confirmed her suspicions. The stranger she'd seen earlier that day might have been a hired hand, a cog in a larger machine, but the true orchestrator, the one with the motive and the local ties, might very well be someone like Danny. Someone who had been chewed up and spit out by Rio Seco, and who was now looking for a way to exact his revenge, using Oakhaven's ingrained rivalry as a shield and a catalyst.

The pieces were starting to fall into place, forming a picture that was both disquieting and, in a strange way, more tangible than the abstract theories she'd been spinning earlier. It wasn't just an outsider with a cryptic message anymore. It was personal. It was rooted in the very soil of Rio Seco, in its history, in its feuds. And if this Danny character was indeed involved, then the trail had indeed heated up, leading her back to the familiar, yet now more complex, landscape of her own hometown's shadows. The County Fair, meant to be a celebration of Rio Seco's resilience, was now also a target, and the metallic orb, once a symbol of renewed pride, was now a pawn in a game of old grudges and inter-town animosity. Esme knew she had to dig deeper, to uncover the specifics of Danny's past in Rio Seco, to understand what had driven him away and what fueled his current animosity. The rivalry between Oakhaven and Rio Seco, a childish game in many ways, had just become a whole lot more serious.

The dim glow of the streetlights cast long, distorted shadows as Esme navigated the familiar route back from Oakhaven. The Oakhaven Omelet had been a hub of whispers, a fertile ground for suspicion, and the encounter with Danny had only solidified her unease. His dismissiveness, his rough edges, and the waitress's telling remarks about his troubled past in Rio Seco painted a vivid picture of a man nursing a deep-seated resentment. But the diner alone wasn't enough. She needed to corroborate what she'd learned, to find someone who might have seen more, someone who could connect the dots she was frantically trying to draw. That's why, instead of heading straight home, she found herself veering off the main road, her skates gliding silently towards the outskirts of town, towards the sprawling, skeletal remains of the old abandoned mill.

She pulled up beside the rusted chain-link fence, the air thick with the scent of damp earth and decaying wood. The mill loomed before her, a silhouette against the bruised twilight sky, its broken windows like vacant eyes staring out into the emptiness. It was a place most people in Rio Seco avoided, a relic of a bygone era, whispered about in hushed tones, associated with everything from asbestos to unhappy spirits. But for Esme, it was a sanctuary of sorts, a place where she could think, where she could escape the suffocating expectations of her small town. And tonight, it was also the meeting place for her most unlikely ally.

A figure detached itself from the deeper shadows near the mill's main entrance. It was Finn. Even in the dim light, his distinctive shock of prematurely grey hair was unmistakable. He approached with a quiet, almost fluid grace, his movements economical and sure. He carried a battered canvas backpack slung over one shoulder, the kind that suggested more than just a casual stroll.

"You made it," Finn's voice was a low rumble, devoid of any surprise. He'd always possessed an unnerving calmness, a quality that Esme found both reassuring and slightly unsettling.

"Wouldn't miss it," Esme replied, her voice catching slightly in the cool night air. She could feel the adrenaline still coursing through her veins from the

Oakhaven trip, the lingering tension from her conversation with Danny. "You said you had something important to tell me."

Finn nodded, his gaze sweeping over her, a silent question in his eyes. "You too. I saw you heading out towards Oakhaven earlier. Everything alright?"

Esme dismounted her skates, leaning them against the fence. "That's what I wanted to talk to you about. I think things are… heating up. Remember that stranger I told you about? The one with the peculiar accent, asking questions about the town's history, about the… exhibit?"

Finn's expression shifted, a flicker of something unreadable crossing his features. "The one you said looked like he'd just stepped out of a spy novel?"

"That's the one," Esme confirmed, her voice dropping as she recounted the details of her encounter. "He was carrying a birdcage. A very specific kind of birdcage, Finn. It was ornate, made of dark, wrought iron, and it had this intricate filigree pattern, almost like a spiderweb. And it wasn't empty. I heard a faint rustling inside, like something small was moving around." She paused, letting the image sink in. "And he knew about the orb. He asked if it had been 'safely stored' yet. It felt… threatening."

Finn listened intently, his brow furrowed in concentration. He pulled a worn notebook and a pen from his backpack, making a few quick notes, his pen scratching softly in the quiet.

"A birdcage," Finn mused aloud. "That's… specific. And the accent. You said it was hard to place?"

"Like he was trying to mask it, but it kept slipping through," Esme elaborated. "And the way he looked at me… it was like he was sizing me up, calculating

something. He also mentioned something about 'connections' between towns, about how history often repeats itself. It sounded like a veiled threat, Finn, or a warning. I don't know which."

"The birdcage, the accent, the questions," Finn repeated, tapping his pen against his notebook. "It all fits with what I saw earlier today. Not in Oakhaven, but here. Closer to home."

Esme's attention snapped back to him. "What did you see?"

"I was out near the old abandoned mill this afternoon," Finn began, his gaze drifting towards the dilapidated structure behind them. "Checking out some of the old drainage systems. Heard there were some rare fungi growing in the damp areas. Anyway, while I was there, I saw a vehicle parked on the access road. It was a dark green van, nondescript, but it had a dented rear bumper that looked distinctive. Looked like it had been in some kind of scrape."

Esme's mind immediately went to the stranger. "A van? Was it the same one you saw near the historical society a few days ago?"

"I believe so," Finn confirmed. "It had that same distinctive bumper. And while I was there, trying to get a better look without being seen, I saw someone walking away from the mill, heading towards the van. It was Danny."

Danny. The name hung in the air, heavy with implication. Danny, the disgruntled former resident of Rio Seco, now seemingly making Oakhaven his base of operations, or at least a place he frequented.

"Danny?" Esme's voice was laced with disbelief and dawning comprehension. "Are you sure?"

"Positive," Finn said, his tone firm. "He was carrying something. A large object, covered with a tarp or a dark cloth. He was struggling with it, trying to get it into the back of the van. He looked agitated, glancing around as if he expected to be seen."

Esme's breath hitched. The covered object. The agitated demeanor. It all lined up with the pieces she'd collected. The stranger, with his cryptic warnings and his birdcage, could be a hired hand, a distraction, or an accomplice. But Danny, with his history in Rio Seco, his apparent newfound ties to Oakhaven, and his suspicious activity near the mill, felt like the linchpin.

"The mill," Esme whispered, the word carrying a new weight. "He was carrying it *towards* the van. Was it… could it have been the orb?"

Finn's eyes met hers, and the shared understanding passed between them. "It's a possibility. It's large enough to be covered like that. And the mill… it's out of the way. A perfect place to hide something, or to make a transfer."

"But why the mill?" Esme mused aloud. "It's not exactly a central location. And what about the birdcage? What does that have to do with Danny and the mill?"

Finn pulled out his notebook again, flipping through a few pages. "I might have an answer for the birdcage. Remember how you said the stranger's accent was hard to place, almost as if he was trying to mask it? And how you felt he was 'calculating' you?"

Esme nodded.

"I remembered something else," Finn continued. "When I was investigating the historical society break-in, I found some odd residue near the display case that had been forced open. It wasn't dust or dirt. It was… fine, metallic particles. And there was a faint, almost imperceptible scent, something herbal, like dried lavender. It was faint, but I remembered it because it was so out of place."

He paused, his gaze fixed on the mill's dark facade. "I did some research. Certain rare bird species, kept in specialized enclosures, require specific environmental conditions. Some of those conditions can involve the use of certain herbs for calming them, or for masking their scent. And the metallic particles… well, ornate metalwork, like intricate filigree on a birdcage, can shed microscopic filings during transport or handling."

Esme stared at him, a shiver tracing its way down her spine. The pieces were snapping together with alarming speed. The stranger, with his birdcage and his cryptic words, and Danny, the disgruntled ex-resident, seen at the abandoned mill with a covered object, potentially the stolen orb. The metallic particles and herbal scent at the historical society, overlooked by the authorities, now potentially linked to the stranger's peculiar prop.

"So," Esme began, her voice barely a whisper, "the stranger might have been casing the historical society, perhaps looking for something specific, or even disabling security. And his birdcage wasn't just a prop, it was… a clue. And Danny, who knows Rio Seco inside and out, who has a motive for wanting to disrupt the town's resurgence… he's involved. He's the one moving the orb, and he's using the mill as a staging ground."

"It seems that way," Finn agreed. "The mill is secluded. It's a place where you could meet someone, make a handover, or even hide something temporarily before moving it on. And Danny's presence there, coupled with what you saw and what I found, paints a clear picture."

"But what was in the birdcage?" Esme pressed, her mind still trying to grapple with the strangeness of it all. "It wasn't just a prop, was it? If it was linked to the historical society break-in, what was he trying to… transport?"

Finn shook his head. "That's the missing piece, the one that still doesn't quite fit. He mentioned 'connections' between towns, and you heard him asking about the orb. The orb is a symbol for Rio Seco. But what if the birdcage, and whatever was inside it, represents something else entirely? Something connected to Oakhaven, or even further afield?"

He looked back at the mill, a newfound intensity in his gaze. "That mill, Esme, it's not just an abandoned building. It's a nexus. It's where your stranger might have met Danny, where the orb might have been moved, and where secrets related to both towns could be hidden."

Esme felt a surge of determination. The vague unease she'd felt when she first heard about the missing mascot had sharpened into a focused intent. This wasn't just about a stolen fair attraction anymore. This was about a deliberate act of sabotage, potentially orchestrated by someone with deep roots in Rio Seco's troubled past, and facilitated by an outsider with an equally mysterious agenda.

"We have to go to the mill," Esme stated, her voice firm. "Now."

Finn didn't hesitate. "I'm with you. But we need to be careful. If Danny is involved, and he's the one moving the orb, he might still be around. Or whoever he's meeting could be."

Esme grabbed her skates, a renewed sense of purpose propelling her. The mystery of the missing orb, the cryptic stranger, the disgruntled ex-resident — it was all converging at this forgotten place, this monument to Rio Seco's industrial past. The shared information, the mutual suspicions, had solidified their alliance. Finn, with his quiet observations and meticulous research, and Esme, with her intuition and her skates, were piecing together a narrative that the authorities had overlooked. The trail hadn't just heated up; it had led them to a dark, silent location, a place where the secrets of Rio Seco and its enigmatic rival might finally be exposed. And Esme, with Finn by her side, was ready

to skate into the heart of that mystery. The abandoned mill was no longer just a landmark; it was the next frontier, a place of potential answers, and she was determined to find them, one silent glide at a time.

The moon, a sliver of bone in the inky sky, offered little illumination as Esme nudged her skates into motion. The familiar asphalt of the deserted county road felt slick and uncertain beneath her wheels, each rotation a whisper against the oppressive silence of the night. The humid air, thick with the scent of pine needles and damp earth, clung to her skin like a second layer, amplifying the prickle of apprehension that had settled in her gut. Finn's words echoed in her mind — the dented green van, Danny's furtive movements, the hulking, tarp-draped object he'd struggled to hoist into the vehicle. The abandoned mill. It was the logical, yet terrifying, next step.

She'd bypassed the town's edge, sticking to the less-trafficked routes that skirted the fringes of Rio Seco, the ones less likely to be patrolled, less likely to have late-night wanderers. The further she went, the more pronounced the rural stillness became. The comforting hum of the town receded, replaced by the rustling of unseen creatures in the undergrowth and the occasional, mournful cry of a distant coyote. Each shadow that stretched across the road seemed to warp and writhe, playing tricks on her eyes, transforming mundane shapes into lurking figures. Her breath hitched with every sudden sound, her senses on high alert, straining to discern genuine threats from the overactive imagination of a teenager on a clandestine mission.

The skates, her usual companions for exploration and escape, now felt like a double-edged sword. They offered speed and silence, an advantage in this covert operation. But they also made her vulnerable, exposed on the open road. She hugged the shoulder, the gravel crunching a sharp counterpoint to the smooth glide of her wheels. The beam of her small, powerful flashlight cut a narrow path through the darkness, bouncing ahead, illuminating patches of asphalt, the skeletal silhouettes of roadside trees, and the occasional glint of dew-kissed spiderwebs strung between blades of grass. It felt like skating through a dream, a disquieting one where the familiar landscape had been transformed into something alien and menacing.

The abandoned mill was a place etched into the local lore of Rio Seco, a ghost story whispered around campfires and in hushed tones in school hallways. It was a relic of the town's boom-and-bust industrial past, a hulking structure that had stood silent and decaying for decades, slowly being reclaimed by nature. Most people gave it a wide berth, associating it with danger – from unstable structures to more superstitious fears of restless spirits. It was precisely that isolation, that reputation for being a place best left undisturbed, that made it the perfect, albeit chilling, destination.

As she drew closer, the air grew colder, the scent of decay more potent, mingling with the metallic tang of rust and stagnant water. The mill itself began to materialize from the gloom, a colossal, skeletal frame against the star-dusted canvas of the sky. Its gaping, broken windows were like vacant sockets in a skull, staring out into the emptiness. Twisted metal beams protruded from the roof like broken ribs, and sections of the brickwork had crumbled, revealing the dark interiors within. It was a monument to abandonment, a silent testament to a forgotten era.

Esme slowed her pace, the wheels of her skates no longer a swift whisper but a hesitant murmur. She scanned the perimeter, her flashlight beam sweeping across the overgrown grounds. The access road Finn had mentioned was barely more than a rutted track, disappearing into a tangle of weeds and brambles. She could see the faint outline of the dark green van, just as Finn had described it, parked incongruously at the edge of the treeline, a jarring modern intrusion on the ancient decay. It sat silent, an ominous presence that amplified the sense of unease.

Skating off the road and onto the softer earth of the overgrown track was a challenge. The wheels sank into the damp soil, slowing her progress, making her feel like she was wading through mud. She dismounted, securing her skates to her backpack. The silence here was profound, broken only by the relentless chirping of crickets and the occasional snap of a twig under some unseen creature's weight. The sheer scale of the mill was more apparent on foot, its imposing mass dwarfing her, a silent sentinel guarding its secrets.

She approached the van cautiously, her flashlight beam darting ahead. The dented bumper was exactly as Finn had described, a jagged scar on the otherwise nondescript vehicle. She circled it slowly, looking for any signs of occupancy, any indication that Danny, or whoever he was meeting, might still be present. The van was locked, its windows dark and impenetrable. The only clue was the faint smell of something acrid, like stale exhaust fumes, clinging to the air around it.

Her gaze was drawn to the main entrance of the mill, a cavernous opening that yawned like a dark mouth. This was where Danny had been seen, emerging from the shadowed interior with his burden. The air around the entrance was thick with the smell of mildew and something else… something vaguely metallic, like old machinery left to rust. She hesitated, her heart thudding against her ribs like a trapped bird. The flashlight beam wavered as her hand trembled slightly.

She took a deep breath, pushing down the rising tide of fear. Finn was waiting, relying on her, and the pieces of the puzzle were too compelling to ignore. The stranger with the birdcage, the unsettling questions, Danny's involvement, and now this silent, hulking mill – it all pointed to something far more significant than a stolen mascot. She had to know what was inside, what Danny had been so desperate to conceal.

Creeping towards the entrance, she kept her movements deliberate, her senses hyper-alert. The ground beneath her feet was a mixture of loose gravel, shattered glass, and decaying debris. The flashlight beam cut through the oppressive darkness, illuminating the cavernous space within. Dust motes danced in the light, disturbed by her intrusion. Old machinery, rusted and immobile, loomed like prehistoric skeletons. Cobwebs, thick as cotton candy, draped from every surface, shimmering eerily in the beam. The air was stagnant, heavy with the scent of rot and the ghosts of industrial labor.

She moved deeper into the mill, her footsteps unnaturally loud in the pervasive quiet. She imagined Danny's struggle, the weight of the object he carried, his furtive glances. Had he been alone? Or had he been waiting for someone, making a clandestine exchange?

The sheer size of the mill offered endless possibilities for hiding, for meeting, for conducting illicit business. Each shadow seemed to hold a secret, each creak of the ancient structure a whispered warning.

Her flashlight beam swept across the vast open floor of the main processing area. There were remnants of conveyor belts, corroded vats, and massive, silent looms, all draped in dust and decay. It was easy to see why people avoided this place. It felt like a tomb, a forgotten monument to a time when this place had thrummed with activity. But now, it was a silent witness.

She reached the spot where Finn had seen Danny. The ground here was disturbed, scuffed by heavy shoes, and there were faint drag marks in the thick layer of dust, consistent with something large being moved. Her flashlight beam followed these marks, leading her further into the mill, towards a darker, more secluded section. This area seemed to be where the raw materials would have been processed, a maze of rusted metal and crumbling brickwork.

The metallic scent was stronger here, mingling with a faint, unpleasant odor that she couldn't quite place – something musky, almost organic. She paused, listening. The crickets still chirped outside, a reassuringly normal sound, but inside, the silence felt different, heavier, pregnant with unseen presences. She swept her flashlight beam upwards, illuminating the decaying roof structure, a complex network of beams and support structures that looked incredibly fragile.

As her light played over the floor, something caught her eye. Near the wall, partially obscured by a fallen beam, was a small, dark object. It was unlike the general debris of the mill. Intrigued, she approached, her heart quickening its pace. It was a piece of fabric, a dark, rough material, snagged on a protruding piece of metal. As she nudged it with the toe of her sneaker, a faint scent wafted up, and for a fleeting moment, she recognized it – the herbal, lavender-like scent Finn had described, the scent he'd found at the historical society.

Her breath hitched. This was it. The connection. The same scent linked to the stranger and his birdcage, now found here, at the scene of Danny's suspicious activity. She carefully knelt, her flashlight held steady, examining the fabric. It was a scrap, no bigger than her hand, dark and coarse. She resisted the urge to touch it, to pocket it. She needed to be thorough, to document, not to contaminate.

Her gaze then fell upon something else, closer to the drag marks. It was a small, metallic glint, almost imperceptible in the dim light. She moved the fallen beam aside, her muscles straining, and revealed a cluster of fine, dark particles, like metallic dust. The same metallic particles Finn had found. This wasn't a coincidence. It was a tangible link, a breadcrumb trail leading from the historical society, through the shadowy presence of the stranger, and directly to this place, to Danny, and to whatever he had been moving.

The pieces were no longer just snapping together; they were interlocking with a decisive click. The stranger hadn't just been a curious observer. His birdcage, his peculiar scent, the metallic dust – they were clues to his presence, and perhaps his involvement in the break-in itself. And Danny, a local with a grievance, was now the courier, the one moving the stolen artifact, using the mill as a waypoint.

But the question of what was inside the birdcage, and what was in the tarp-draped object Danny had moved, remained. The scent and dust suggested the stranger had been in close proximity to whatever he carried, perhaps transporting it in that ornate cage. And Danny's object, large enough to be concealed, felt intrinsically linked to this. Was it the orb itself, or something else entirely, something the stranger was meant to receive or transport?

Esme's flashlight beam continued its sweep, illuminating more of the mill's vast interior. She moved with a newfound sense of urgency, her earlier apprehension now overshadowed by a burning curiosity. The sheer scale of the place was daunting, but she was committed. She had to explore every corner, every shadow.

She ventured deeper into the labyrinthine structure, her flashlight beam probing the darkness. She passed by rows of smaller rooms, offices perhaps, their doors long gone, their interiors filled with the detritus of years of neglect. Broken furniture, scattered papers turned to pulp, and the pervasive scent of decay. It was a silent testament to the people who had once worked here, their lives now reduced to echoes in the dust.

She found a set of crumbling stairs, leading upwards to what must have been a second level. Hesitantly, she ascended, testing each step before committing her weight. The wooden treads groaned ominously underfoot, threatening to give way. The air grew mustier, heavier. The second level seemed to be a network of catwalks and platforms, overlooking the main floor, offering a different perspective on the decaying machinery below.

From this vantage point, she could see more clearly the extent of the mill's disrepair. Sections of the floor had collapsed entirely, leaving gaping holes that plunged into the darkness below. The metal catwalks were pitted with rust, and she could feel them sway slightly with her movements. It was a treacherous environment, a stark reminder of the dangers she was willingly courting.

Her flashlight beam caught something on a rickety table on one of the catwalks. It was a ledger, its cover warped and stained, its pages fused together by damp. She approached it carefully, her gloved hand reaching out to gently touch its brittle surface. It felt ancient, fragile. She resisted the urge to open it, fearing it would disintegrate at her touch. This mill held more than just a stolen artifact; it held history, secrets, and the unspoken stories of those who had once toiled within its walls.

The thought of the orb, the stolen mascot, felt almost trivial now, a catalyst for uncovering a much larger, more complex web of intrigue. The stranger's birdcage, the metallic particles, the herbal scent, Danny's clandestine activities – they were all pieces of a puzzle that extended beyond Rio Seco's borders, hinted at by the stranger's comments about "connections" between towns.

As she continued her silent exploration, a sudden, sharp noise echoed from somewhere within the mill. It was a metallic clang, followed by a scraping sound, as if something heavy had been dragged across concrete. Esme froze, her breath catching in her throat. The sound was not from outside, but from deeper within the mill, from a section she hadn't yet explored.

Her flashlight beam whipped around, searching the shadows. The crickets outside seemed to have fallen silent, leaving an even more profound stillness. The adrenaline that had been a low hum now surged, a cold, sharp spike of fear. Was Danny still here? Or had he returned with someone else?

She moved cautiously towards the source of the sound, her senses on high alert. The drag marks and the metallic dust were more concentrated in this area, leading towards a large, rusted metal door set into the far wall. The door was partially ajar, revealing an even deeper, blacker void beyond. The unpleasant, musky odor was strongest here, almost suffocating.

With a surge of desperate courage, Esme pushed the heavy metal door open further. It groaned in protest, a long, drawn-out shriek that seemed to reverberate through the entire structure. The beam of her flashlight cut through the absolute darkness of the room beyond, revealing a small, concrete chamber. It was sparsely furnished, with nothing but a few overturned crates and a large, tarp-covered object lying on the floor.

And then she saw it. Lying on the tarp, near the object, was an empty, ornate birdcage, its dark wrought iron gleaming dully in the flashlight beam. It was identical to the one she had described to Finn. The intricate filigree, the spiderweb-like pattern – it was unmistakable. And beside it, lying discarded, was a small, dark cloth bag, the kind one might use to carry fragile items, perhaps something small and living.

Her heart hammered against her ribs. The stranger's birdcage, right here. And the object beneath the tarp… it was large, substantial. She stepped closer, her flashlight beam unwavering. As she reached out to pull back the tarp, a voice, rough and low, echoed from the shadows behind her.

"Looking for something?"

5: Confrontation and Revelation

The metallic clang, sharp and jarring, echoed through the vast, skeletal remains of the mill, shattering the fragile silence. Esme froze, her flashlight beam cutting a desperate arc through the dust-laden air. The sound hadn't been a creak of decaying metal or the rustle of unseen vermin. It was the unmistakable sound of something heavy being dropped, or perhaps, moved with a careless disregard for its surroundings. Her breath hitched, a shallow, ragged sound in the overwhelming quiet. The crickets, which had been a constant, almost comforting soundtrack to her solitary exploration, seemed to have fallen utterly silent, as if they too sensed the intrusion.

She was deep within the mill now, the entrance a distant memory, swallowed by the labyrinthine corridors of rusted machinery and collapsed walkways. The air, already thick with the scent of mildew and stagnant water, now carried a new, more potent aroma – a musky, almost animalistic odor, mingled with the sharp, acrid tang of something that spoke of recent, deliberate activity. It was a smell that prickled at her senses, raising the hairs on the back of her neck, a visceral warning that she was no longer alone in this forgotten edifice.

Her skates, a sleek silver blur against the grimy concrete floor, had been her silent allies, allowing her to traverse the vast expanse of the mill with a ghost-like stealth. They glided effortlessly over the thick carpets of dust, the accumulated detritus of decades, barely disturbing the layers of decay. Each rotation of her wheels was a whisper against the palpable silence, a stark contrast to the heavy thuds and scrapes that now emanated from deeper within the structure.

She moved with agonizing slowness, her flashlight beam, a powerful, focused shaft of light, probing the oppressive darkness ahead. The main processing floor, where massive, silent looms and corroded vats stood like ancient monoliths, was a stark tableau of industrial ruin. Dust motes danced in her beam, disturbed by her almost imperceptible movements, creating phantom shapes in the gloom. Cobwebs, thick and intricate, draped from every beam and girder, shimmering like spectral curtains in the artificial light.

The drag marks Finn had described, faint but discernible in the thick dust, were more pronounced here, leading her towards a section of the mill that seemed even more secluded, more deliberately hidden. They spoke of a struggle, of something heavy and unwieldy being hauled across the rough concrete, its passage leaving a trail of disturbed history. It was in this area that the metallic scent Finn had noted, the same scent she'd detected clinging to the fabric scrap and the metallic particles, was strongest.

She paused, listening intently. The sounds had stopped. The silence that rushed back in was more unnerving than the noise itself, a heavy, expectant hush that seemed to swallow all other ambient sounds. It was the silence of a predator, waiting, observing. Had Danny returned? Or had whoever he was meeting decided to make an appearance? Her mind raced, conjuring images of shadowy figures, of clandestine transactions.

Her flashlight beam, trembling slightly in her unsteady hand, swept across the floor. The drag marks led her to a cluster of overturned crates near the far wall, their wooden surfaces splintered and aged. And then, her light caught something that made her breath catch in her throat. It was a discarded food wrapper, a garish splash of color against the muted tones of decay, and next to it, a half-empty bottle of water. Recent. Definitely recent. Someone had been here, and not long ago.

But it was what lay beyond the crates that truly drew her attention. Partially obscured by a fallen section of corrugated metal roofing, was a large, wooden crate. It was unlike the general debris of the mill, its edges sharp, its surface surprisingly free of the thickest layer of dust, as if it had been placed there relatively recently. It seemed incongruous, out of place amidst the pervasive rot and decay. The drag marks led directly to it, suggesting it was the object of the struggle.

A wave of dizziness washed over her, a potent cocktail of fear and exhilaration. She was so close. The pieces, so disparate and confusing just hours before, were coalescing, forming a picture far more complex and sinister than she had ever imagined. The stolen mascot, the ornate birdcage, the stranger with the unusual scent, Danny's furtive actions, and now this mill, this silent, decaying monument to industry, revealing its secrets under the cloak of night.

She skates off the main floor, her movements slow and deliberate, approaching the crate. The wood was rough, weathered, but the sheer size of it was imposing. It was far too large to be a simple piece of equipment from the mill. It felt… manufactured. Portable, perhaps, but designed to contain something substantial. She circled it, her flashlight beam meticulously examining every inch. There were no markings, no labels, nothing to indicate its contents or its origin.

The musky scent was strongest here, emanating from the crate itself, or perhaps from whatever was contained within it. It was a cloying, almost sickly sweet aroma, overlaid with the faint, metallic tang she'd come to associate with the stranger. This was the nexus, the point where all the disparate threads of her investigation converged.

She knelt beside the crate, her skates making tiny scraping sounds on the concrete that seemed impossibly loud. She leaned closer, her ear almost touching the rough wood, straining to hear any sound from within. Nothing. Only the muffled thumping of her own heart, a frantic drumbeat against her ribs.

Then, her flashlight beam caught something else, nestled in the dust beside the crate. It was a small, metal object, tarnished and dull, like a piece of old hardware. She picked it up, turning it over in her gloved fingers. It was a hinge. A small, ornate hinge, not the sort one would find on a typical shipping crate. It was the kind of detail, the kind of craftsmanship, that spoke of something more refined, more… precious.

Her mind immediately flashed back to the description of the birdcage Finn had given her. The intricate metalwork, the almost delicate construction. Could this hinge be from the same craftsman? And if so, what did it imply about the contents of this crate? Was it possible that the stolen mascot wasn't a mascot at all, but something far more significant, something requiring such careful, and expensive, transport?

The silence of the mill pressed in on her, vast and suffocating. She felt like a tiny speck of dust adrift in an ocean of forgotten time. The courage that had propelled her here, the burning curiosity, warred with a rising tide of primal fear. She was an intruder, a trespasser in a place that held secrets far older and perhaps more dangerous than she could comprehend.

The thought of Finn waiting, of his unwavering trust in her, spurred her onward. She couldn't turn back now. She had to know what was inside this crate. She looked around for something to pry it open, her gaze falling on a thick, rusted metal pipe lying nearby. It was heavy, solid, a tool of brute force in this otherwise silent excavation.

As she reached for the pipe, another sound echoed through the mill. This one was different. A shuffling, a dragging sound, closer now, and accompanied by a low, guttural murmur. It was the sound of movement, of hushed, urgent speech. Someone was definitely here.

Esme dropped the pipe instantly, her movements fluid and instinctive. She flattened herself against the wall behind a massive, defunct piece of machinery, her flashlight beam extinguished, plunging her into near-total darkness. The only light was the faint, diffused moonlight filtering through the shattered windows high above, casting long, distorted shadows that danced and writhed with every subtle shift in the air currents.

She held her breath, straining her ears. The shuffling grew louder, closer. She could hear the crunch of footsteps on the dusty floor, the uneven rhythm of someone trying to move stealthily, but failing. The musky scent, now mingled with a faint, earthy aroma, seemed to intensify, clinging to the air like a shroud.

Then, she saw them. Silhouetted against the faint moonlight filtering through a gaping hole in the wall, two figures emerged from the gloom. They were tall, bulky, their movements slow and deliberate as they wrestled with another large object, this one covered in a dark, coarse canvas. It was smaller than the crate she had discovered, but still substantial.

Esme's heart hammered against her ribs, a frantic, trapped bird. She recognized one of the figures. It was Danny. His shoulders were hunched, his movements strained as he helped his companion maneuver the canvas-wrapped object. The other figure was a stranger, a broad-shouldered man whose face was obscured by the shadows and the low-brimmed cap he wore.

They were bringing something *else* into the mill. Something Danny was actively involved in transporting. The crate, the hinge, the footprints, the food wrapper – it all began to slot into a terrifyingly coherent narrative. Danny wasn't just moving something for someone else; he was part of a larger operation, a local connection facilitating the movement of these mysterious items.

She watched, paralyzed, as they dragged the canvas-wrapped object towards a section of the mill she hadn't yet explored, a darker, more cavernous area at the far end of the processing floor, where the shadows clung like a second skin. They passed within feet of her hiding place, and she could feel the vibrations of their footsteps through the concrete floor. The musky scent was almost overwhelming now, a suffocating presence.

She heard Danny grunt with effort, then a low, indistinct mumble from the stranger. It was impossible to make out what they were saying, their voices muffled by the vastness of the mill and the thick dust. But their actions were eloquent enough. They were securing something, hiding something, in the deepest recesses of this derelict building.

Once they had disappeared into the deeper shadows, Esme waited, counting to a hundred, her muscles aching from the tension. The silence returned, broken only by the frantic thumping of her own pulse. She risked a peek from behind the machinery. The two figures were gone. But the canvas-wrapped object remained, a dark, ominous lump against the dusty floor.

Her initial plan, to investigate the crate, was now overshadowed by a more urgent need. She had to see what Danny and his companion had brought. The risk had multiplied tenfold, but so had her determination. She had stumbled upon a secret, a clandestine operation happening under her town's nose, and she was not about to let it remain hidden.

She emerged from her hiding place, moving with a newfound urgency. Her skates, now a tool for speed rather than stealth, carried her swiftly across the floor towards the canvas-wrapped object. As she drew closer, the earthy scent intensified, and she could discern a faint, rhythmic pulsing coming from within the bundle. It was a subtle vibration, a low thrum that resonated deep within her bones.

She reached the object, her hand trembling as she reached out to touch the rough canvas. It was cool to the touch, and the pulsing sensation grew stronger. What was inside? A machine? Some kind of device? The ornate hinge, the large crate – it was all starting to feel connected to something far more significant than a stolen school mascot. This was bigger than Rio Seco, bigger than their small town drama.

Her flashlight beam, now re-ignited, played over the canvas. She noticed a small tear near the bottom, a ragged opening that offered a tantalizing glimpse of what lay beneath. She hesitated for a moment, her breath catching in her throat. This was it. The point of no return. The revelation she had been seeking, hidden in the heart of this forgotten mill.

With a surge of adrenaline, she knelt and carefully pulled back the torn section of canvas. The beam of her flashlight sliced into the darkness within, revealing… feathers. A cascade of dark, iridescent feathers, shimmering even in the dim light. They were soft, downy, and arranged in a way that suggested a living creature nestled within.

Esme blinked, her mind struggling to process what her eyes were seeing. Feathers. Not just any feathers, but large, magnificent ones. They were the color of midnight, with hints of deep sapphire and emerald woven through them. And then, she saw it. The distinct shape of a head, resting on delicate, folded wings. It was an animal, something large and exotic, sleeping or perhaps sedated, bundled tightly in the canvas.

The musky, earthy scent suddenly made a horrifying kind of sense. It was the scent of an animal, perhaps something from a distant land, something kept in captivity. And the ornate birdcage, the large crate, the meticulous packaging – it all pointed to a creature of immense value, or perhaps, of immense importance.

Her gaze swept back to the large wooden crate she had discovered earlier. The hinges, the sheer size – could it be its enclosure? Had Danny and his accomplice been transporting not one, but two creatures? Or perhaps the crate was for something else entirely, something the stranger needed to transport, and this animal was a separate element of the operation.

She felt a growing unease, a chilling realization that this was far more than a simple theft. The secrecy, the clandestine movements, the exotic creature – it suggested something far more organized, something potentially illegal, and definitely dangerous. The stranger's comments about "connections" echoed in her mind. What kind of connections involved transporting exotic animals through abandoned mills in the dead of night?

Suddenly, a floorboard creaked from somewhere behind her, a sharp, undeniable sound that snapped her out of her stunned observation. She whipped her head around, her flashlight beam darting towards the source of the noise. The darkness seemed to deepen, to press in on her from all sides. The silence was absolute once more, save for the frantic pounding of her own heart.

She scrambled to her feet, her skates making a soft whisper as she rose. She scanned the surrounding machinery, her breath coming in ragged gasps. Had they returned? Had they heard her? The thought sent a fresh wave of terror through her. She was exposed, vulnerable, caught red-handed in the midst of their operation.

The shuffling sound came again, closer this time, accompanied by a low, menacing growl. It wasn't human. Esme's blood ran cold. The growl was deep, resonant, and utterly terrifying. It was the sound of a predator, a large predator, and it was coming from the direction of the canvas-wrapped bundle.

She realized, with a sickening lurch of her stomach, that the creature was not sedated. It was awake. And it was agitated. The rhythmic pulsing she had felt earlier was the frantic beat of its heart, or perhaps the movement of its muscles beneath the canvas.

Panic began to set in, a cold, creeping dread. She was trapped between the large crate and the newly revealed creature, with the possibility of Danny and his accomplice lurking in the shadows. Her skates, her usual means of escape, felt like a liability on the rough, uneven floor.

She had to get out. Now. But as she turned to flee, her flashlight beam caught a glint of metal near the canvas. It was another piece of equipment, a heavy-duty restraint, a thick chain secured to a metal anchor point hammered into the concrete floor. This wasn't just an animal being transported; it was a dangerous one, a creature that required such extreme measures to control.

The growl intensified, a low rumble that vibrated through the very concrete beneath her feet. The canvas rustled violently, as if the creature was struggling against its bonds. Esme took a step back, her eyes wide with terror, her mind racing for an escape route. The mill, once a place of silent secrets, had become a den of dangerous revelations, and she was caught in its heart. The thrill of discovery had curdled into pure, unadulterated fear. She had found the missing pieces, but the puzzle they formed was far more terrifying than she could have ever imagined.

The air in the mill grew heavier, denser, as Esme ventured further from the relative openness of the main floor. Dust motes, disturbed by her passage, swirled in the beam of her flashlight, creating ephemeral constellations in the gloom. The silence, punctuated only by the soft whir of her skates, was a living entity, pressing in on her, amplifying every subtle shift in the oppressive atmosphere. She had moved past the overturned crates, the discarded wrapper, the ominous canvas-wrapped bundle that still pulsed with an unsettling, unseen life. Her focus, however, had been drawn by something far more subtle, yet infinitely more significant.

It had begun as a whisper, a faint percussive rhythm against the overwhelming quiet. At first, she'd dismissed it as the settling of the old structure, the groans of ancient metal protesting its decay. But as she moved deeper, navigating a narrow corridor lined with corroded pipes that dripped a viscous, dark liquid, the sound solidified, sharpening into something undeniably familiar. A faint, rhythmic *rattle*.

Her breath hitched. She knew that sound. It was the distinctive, almost musical *clatter* of the armadillo mascot's intricately designed shell, the hollow metallic echo that had been so prominent in the security footage Finn had shown her. It was a sound that had been etched into her memory during her investigation, a sonic signature that had become inextricably linked to the mystery.

The sound seemed to emanate from a section of the mill she hadn't yet explored, a part that felt more secluded, more deliberately hidden. The narrow corridor she was in opened into a wider space, a junction of sorts, where several smaller doorways branched off. One of them, a simple wooden door painted a faded industrial grey, seemed to be the source. The rattling was faint, almost imperceptible if she wasn't actively listening for it, but it was there, a persistent, metallic murmur.

A tremor of anticipation, sharp and exhilarating, shot through her. This was it. The confirmation she'd been desperately seeking. The armadillo wasn't just stolen; it was here, within the confines of this decaying behemoth. The pieces of the puzzle, so scattered and elusive, were finally clicking into place, forming a picture that was both terrifying and undeniably real.

She moved towards the grey door, her skates gliding silently over the grit and grime. Each rotation of her wheels felt like a step closer to the heart of the mystery. The rattling grew slightly louder, a more defined series of clicks and scrapes, as if something was being shifted, or perhaps, as if the mascot itself was subtly moving.

Her flashlight beam swept across the door. It was old, weathered, its paint peeling in long, curling strips. There was no handle, only a simple, rusted latch. It looked like it led to a storage room, or perhaps a maintenance closet, a forgotten corner of the mill's vast industrial landscape.

She paused before the door, her hand hovering over the latch. The sound continued, a soft, almost playful jingle that belied the grim atmosphere of the mill. It was a sound that belonged to the daylight, to the cheering crowds, to the very heart of Rio Seco High.

Here, in the suffocating darkness, it felt like a ghostly echo, a siren song luring her into deeper peril.

She could feel her heart hammering against her ribs, a frenetic rhythm that seemed to synchronize with the faint rattling beyond the door. Fear was a cold knot in her stomach, but it was tempered by an overwhelming surge of determination. She had come too far to turn back now. Finn was counting on her. The town was counting on her.

With a deep breath, she pushed the latch. It groaned in protest, a harsh metallic shriek that momentarily drowned out the rattling. The door swung inward with a slow, creaking protest, revealing a small, cramped space.

Her flashlight beam cut through the darkness, illuminating a surprisingly tidy, albeit dusty, room. Unlike the chaotic disarray of the main mill, this space felt almost… preserved. There were shelves lining the walls, sparsely populated with old tools and empty metal canisters. In the center of the room, dominating the space, sat a large, heavy-duty wooden crate, similar in size and construction to the one she had discovered earlier, but this one was different. This one was clearly sealed with thick, reinforced metal bands and bore a single, stark symbol stenciled onto its side: a stylized, angular bird.

And perched precariously on top of this crate, almost as an afterthought, was the source of the sound.

It was the armadillo.

Or rather, a significant portion of it. Its signature metallic shell, intricately crafted and designed to mimic the animal's natural armor, was visible. The familiar, segmented plates were dulled by a fine layer of dust, but the distinctive shape was unmistakable. And as Esme's beam of light settled upon it, the shell *shifted*. A faint *clatter* sounded as one of the plates settled against another. It wasn't the mascot itself, not the entire, fully assembled creature, but a crucial part of it, its iconic shell.

Her mind reeled. Why was it here, disassembled, sitting atop this mysterious crate? The creature she had seen earlier, wrapped in canvas, was large, powerful, and clearly dangerous. Was this shell meant for it? Or was the mascot simply being used as a cover, a convenient way to transport something far more sinister?

The grey door had swung shut behind her, muffling the sounds of the mill, but the rattling, now amplified by the enclosed space, was clearer than ever. It was a symphony of metallic clicks and whispers, a testament to the intricate craftsmanship of the mascot, and a stark indicator of its presence.

She stepped further into the room, her skates moving with an almost reverent slowness. The air here was different, too. Less humid, less thick with the scent of decay. There was a faint, almost imperceptible aroma of ozone, a sharp, electric tang that prickled at her nostrils. It was a scent she had noticed before, a subtle undercurrent in the overall atmosphere of the mill, but here, in this confined space, it was more pronounced.

Her flashlight beam swept across the crate. It was incredibly sturdy, its wood dark and unblemished, clearly designed for heavy-duty transport. The metal bands were thick, almost like those used to secure industrial machinery. And the stenciled bird symbol… it was stylized, almost abstract, but eerily familiar. She couldn't quite place it, but it evoked a sense of something ancient, something predatory.

She knelt beside the crate, her gaze fixed on the armadillo shell. It was larger than she remembered, more imposing. The intricate detailing on each plate was a work of art, a testament to the skill of its creator. She reached out, her gloved finger tracing the edge of one of the plates. It was cool and smooth to the touch, despite the dust.

The rattling stopped abruptly.

The sudden silence was deafening, more jarring than any sound. Esme froze, her hand still resting on the shell. The abrupt cessation of the noise sent a fresh wave of alarm through her. Had she disturbed something? Or had someone heard her enter?

She strained her ears, listening intently. The only sound was the frantic thumping of her own heart, a desperate drumbeat against the overwhelming quiet. The ozone scent seemed to intensify, making her head swim slightly.

Then, she heard it. Not a rattle this time, but a low, metallic *scrape*. It came from *within* the crate. A slow, deliberate movement, like something heavy being dragged across a rough surface.

Her breath hitched. The armadillo shell, sitting on top of the crate, was merely a decoy, a prop. The real secret, the true purpose of this clandestine operation, was hidden within the reinforced container below.

Her mind raced. The canvas-wrapped creature, the meticulous packaging, the heavy-duty crate with the bird symbol, and now this internal scraping sound. It all pointed to something far more complex and dangerous than a stolen school mascot. The armadillo shell was merely a piece of the puzzle, a piece placed strategically to misdirect, or perhaps, to conceal something else entirely.

She looked around the small room, her flashlight beam darting from shelf to shelf. There had to be something here, some clue to the nature of the contents of the crate, some explanation for the unsettling sounds and smells. The tools on the shelves looked old, standard maintenance equipment. Nothing that would explain the ozone, or the peculiar scraping sound.

But as her beam swept across the back wall, it caught something nestled between two large, empty canisters. It was a small, metal box, no bigger than her hand. It was tarnished and dulled, but its shape was distinct – a small, electronic device, perhaps a communication unit or a sensor. And beside it, almost hidden in the shadows, lay a single, dark, iridescent feather. Not like the feathers of a common bird. These were larger, more exotic, with a sheen that hinted at vibrant colors unseen in the dim light.

Her gaze flicked back to the canvas-wrapped creature she had seen earlier, the one that had been hauled into the mill by Danny and his accomplice. Had that creature shed this feather? And if so, what was its connection to the armadillo shell, and to this heavily reinforced crate?

The scraping sound from within the crate stopped. A moment of tense silence followed, then a soft, rhythmic *thump-thump… thump-thump…* began. It was a low, resonant beat, like a powerful engine starting up, or a massive heart beginning to pump. The ozone smell grew stronger, and a faint vibration emanated from the crate, traveling up through the floor and into the soles of her skates.

Esme felt a prickle of unease, a growing dread that this was far beyond anything she had anticipated. The armadillo, the shell, the creature, the crate – they were all part of a larger, more sinister design. The rattling clue had led her to the heart of the operation, but what she was finding was far more disturbing than she could have ever imagined. The confrontation Finn had predicted was looming, and it was becoming clear that the stakes were exponentially higher than a mere high school mascot. She was no longer just an investigator; she was an intruder in a world of secrets that stretched far beyond the familiar streets of Rio Seco. The familiar rattle had been a beacon, but it had led her into a darkness far deeper and more dangerous than she had ever conceived.

The silence in the small room was a fragile thing, easily shattered. Esme's gaze, sharp and assessing, swept over the contents, piecing together the narrative that the carefully placed fragments were beginning to tell. The metallic scent of ozone still hung heavy in the air, a tangible reminder of the strange power she sensed emanating from the sealed crate. The rhythmic thumping had subsided, leaving behind an unnerving stillness that spoke of an alien kind of anticipation. She had found the armadillo shell, a tantalizing clue, but her instincts screamed that it was merely a decoy, a prop in a much larger, far more dangerous play. The true prize, the real objective, lay hidden within the reinforced walls of the crate.

Her flashlight beam settled on the small, metal box nestled between the canisters. It was nondescript, perhaps a communication device, or some sort of portable power source. Beside it, the dark, iridescent feather seemed to absorb the scant light, its subtle sheen hinting at origins far beyond the familiar avian population of Rio Seco. This feather, she felt with a certainty that chilled her to the bone, was a connection. A connection to the unseen occupant of the canvas-wrapped bundle, and, by extension, to the architects of this elaborate scheme.

But how did this connect to the armadillo? The intricate shell, perched so deliberately atop the crate, felt like a deliberate misdirection. It was a symbol of Rio Seco, of its identity, of the very spirit of the town. Its disappearance had sent ripples of unease through the community, a loss that resonated far beyond its monetary value. Yet, here it was, disassembled, its purpose here unclear. Was it simply a means to an end? A way to draw attention, to create a diversion while something else, something far more valuable or dangerous, was being transported or assembled?

Esme's mind, sharp and analytical, began to weave the threads together. The abandoned mill, a relic of Rio Seco's industrial past, had become the perfect clandestine operational base. Its isolation and decay provided the anonymity needed for illicit activities. She remembered Finn's earlier observations about the security footage, the subtle anomalies that suggested a deliberate manipulation of the cameras, a careful orchestration of the armadillo's disappearance. This wasn't a random act of vandalism; it was a meticulously planned operation.

Her gaze drifted to the discarded notes she had glimpsed near the canvas-wrapped bundle in the main mill. She hadn't had time to examine them closely then, her attention drawn by the rattling sound. Now, a surge of urgency propelled her back towards the corridor. She needed more. She needed to understand the 'who' and the 'why.'

Retracing her steps with a renewed sense of purpose, Esme moved back into the main space of the mill, her flashlight beam cutting through the oppressive gloom. The canvas-wrapped bundle was still there, a silent, ominous presence. Beside it, scattered across the grimy concrete floor, were several crumpled sheets of paper, as if dropped in haste or discarded carelessly.

She knelt, her skates gliding smoothly, and carefully picked up the nearest sheet. The paper was thin, cheap, and covered in hurried, almost frantic handwriting. The ink was a stark black, some of it smudged as if by damp hands. As she scanned the words, a chilling realization began to dawn.

"County Fair deadline… essential to isolate… maximum disruption… public humiliation… leverage secured…"

The phrases were disjointed, fragmented, but their implication was clear. The armadillo wasn't just stolen; it was being held hostage. The timing of its disappearance, coinciding with the upcoming county fair, was no accident. The fair was the town's biggest event, a celebration of its identity and its community spirit. To have the mascot missing during such an important occasion would undoubtedly cause embarrassment and diminish the celebratory atmosphere.

Esme's fingers trembled slightly as she reached for the next sheet. This one contained more detailed financial notations and cryptic references to "payments," "transportation," and "containment units." There were dates, times, and what looked like coded designations for various pieces of equipment. It was a ledger of sorts, meticulously documenting the logistics of their operation.

"Subject secured. Birdcage effective for transit. Minimal structural damage. Stranger handling final deployment."

Birdcage. The word echoed in her mind. She recalled seeing a large, sturdy cage-like structure in the footage Finn had shown her, used to transport the armadillo initially. It was designed to hold something large and robust, but also to allow for ventilation and observation. It made a twisted kind of sense. The cage was used for the initial acquisition and transport, but what about the current phase of the operation? The crate?

The third sheet of paper offered a more personal, and far more disturbing, insight. The handwriting here was different, more deliberate, laced with a bitter resentment.

"Always overlooked. The 'expert' they discarded. Rio Seco owes me. This town built on my father's labor, and they forgot. They forgot him, and they forgot me. The fair will be a reminder. A reminder of what happens when you cast aside those who built you."

This was it. The 'who.' The mastermind. Someone with a deep-seated grievance against Rio Seco, someone who felt wronged and forgotten. The mention of a father and discarded expertise pointed towards a local connection, someone intimately familiar with the town's history and its people. The bitterness in the writing was palpable, a venom that had festered for years.

Esme's mind flashed to the old abandoned workshops on the outskirts of town, places that once housed the town's industrial heart. Places that had fallen into disuse as the economy shifted. She thought of families who had worked in those industries for generations, some of whom had seen their livelihoods disappear.

And then, the 'stranger.' The cryptic mention of a 'stranger handling final deployment' and the fact that she had seen an unknown individual with Danny in the footage, the one who had seemed to be the muscle, the hired help. This stranger was the operative, the one carrying out the plan, likely hired by the disgruntled local. The feather, the ozone smell, the vibrating crate — these were clues to the nature of what the stranger was actually deploying, or perhaps, what was being built or contained within that reinforced crate.

She carefully gathered the scattered notes, her gloved hands treating them like fragile artifacts. The pieces were falling into place with a terrifying clarity. The former resident, fueled by a potent cocktail of resentment and a desire for revenge, had orchestrated the theft of the armadillo. Their motive was to cause maximum embarrassment and disruption during the county fair, a symbolic act of retribution against the town that had, in their eyes, wronged them. The plan involved using the armadillo as a pawn, its disappearance creating a spectacle of public humiliation.

But the scale of the operation suggested something more than just a symbolic gesture. The reinforced crate, the specialized transport, the mysterious feather, and the lingering ozone scent – these elements hinted at a secondary, perhaps even primary, objective that was far more significant than the mascot itself. Was the armadillo shell merely a cover for the transport of something illegal? Something dangerous? Or was the armadillo's mechanical heart, its intricate inner workings, being repurposed for some other, more sinister purpose?

Esme felt a chill creep up her spine. The meticulous planning, the calculated execution, the sheer audacity of the scheme spoke of a mind that was both brilliant and deeply disturbed. The former resident was not just seeking petty revenge; they were aiming for a significant impact, a lasting stain on Rio Seco's reputation. And the hired stranger was the facilitator, the skilled hands that carried out the dirty work.

She looked back towards the small room where she had found the armadillo shell. The crate remained, a silent sentinel of secrets. The 'birdcage' had been the means of transport for the armadillo, but the current situation, with the reinforced crate and its unsettling contents, suggested a more advanced stage of whatever the operation entailed. Was the stranger assembling something? Or was the crate itself a containment unit for something acquired through other means, with the armadillo merely a distraction?

The rough, hasty notes she held were a window into the mind of the perpetrator, revealing a deep-seated anger that had been simmering for years, waiting for the opportune moment to erupt. The county fair was the chosen stage, the armadillo the central prop in a play of humiliation. But the supporting cast – the strange feather, the ozone scent, the powerful vibrations from the crate – spoke of a much darker, more complex narrative unfolding beneath the surface.

Esme's observational prowess, honed by her persistent curiosity and her knack for spotting the seemingly insignificant details, had led her to this derelict mill, to this hidden chamber of secrets. She had followed the trail of discarded clues, from the initial sightings of the armadillo's disassembly to the cryptic sounds and smells that permeated the air. The rattling had been her guide, a sonic breadcrumb trail leading her to the heart of the conspiracy.

The former resident's plan was audacious: to leverage the town's most cherished symbol for maximum embarrassment. By holding the armadillo until after the county fair, they ensured that Rio Seco would have to face its celebratory weekend without its iconic mascot, a visible symbol of their community's spirit. This public spectacle of absence would serve as a constant reminder of the town's perceived failings, a living monument to the perpetrator's grievance.

The ransom aspect was also a crucial piece of the puzzle. Extortion would be a logical extension of holding the mascot hostage. A hefty sum of money, demanded in exchange for its safe return, would not only provide financial gain but also serve as a final, humiliating admission of defeat for the town council and its leaders. It was a calculated move, designed to inflict maximum damage on Rio Seco's pride and its coffers.

Esme felt a surge of adrenaline. She had the 'who' and the 'why,' and she had a clear understanding of the immediate plan. The former resident, driven by a desire for revenge and public humiliation, had hired a skilled operative – the stranger – to carry out the meticulous details of the theft and subsequent holding of the armadillo. The 'birdcage' was the initial transport method, but the reinforced crate suggested a more advanced phase of whatever this operation truly entailed. The feather and the ozone were still lingering questions, hinting at a deeper, more disturbing layer to the scheme that she had yet to fully comprehend.

Her mind raced, replaying the security footage Finn had shown her. Danny and the stranger, their faces obscured by shadows and the grainy quality of the video, moving the armadillo with a practiced efficiency. The way they handled it, with a carefulness that suggested they knew its intricate construction, its delicate mechanics. It wasn't just a joyride; it was a professional operation.

The implications of this discovery were immense. The county fair was rapidly approaching, and Rio Seco was unknowingly walking into a carefully orchestrated humiliation. The town needed to be warned. But how?

Going to the authorities with these fragmented notes and a story about a mysterious feather and ozone smell might be met with skepticism. She needed more concrete evidence, something undeniable that would expose the full extent of the plot.

Esme carefully placed the incriminating notes into a sealed plastic bag she had brought with her, a precaution she had learned was essential when handling sensitive evidence. Her flashlight beam swept across the small room again, lingering on the reinforced crate. The low, rhythmic thumping had ceased, but the sense of latent power remained. What was inside that crate? Was it simply the disassembled armadillo, waiting to be put back together and returned, perhaps after a ransom was paid? Or was it something far more sinister, something the armadillo was merely a distraction from, or a component of?

The former resident's words echoed in her mind: "maximum disruption," "public humiliation," "leverage secured." The armadillo was the lever, and the county fair was the fulcrum. But the stranger's involvement, coupled with the unexplained elements, suggested that the true nature of the operation might extend beyond mere mascot theft and extortion.

She looked at the armadillo shell again, its polished metallic plates dulled by dust. It was a marvel of engineering, a testament to the town's ingenuity. To see it disassembled like this, used as a piece in someone's twisted game, felt like a violation.

Her skates glided silently as she moved back towards the entrance of the small room, her mind already formulating a plan. She had uncovered the core of the conspiracy, the motive, and the individuals involved, at least by description. Now came the crucial part: gathering irrefutable proof and ensuring that Rio Seco wouldn't be blindsided at its most important celebration. The confrontation Finn had warned her about was no longer a distant possibility; it was an imminent reality, and Esme found herself standing at its precipice, armed with the truth, and facing a darkness far more complex than she had ever imagined. The fate of the county fair, and perhaps much more, rested on her ability to act decisively on the knowledge she had so painstakingly uncovered.

The faint scent of ozone, clinging stubbornly to the air in the abandoned mill, seemed to intensify as Esme carefully gathered the crumpled notes. Each sheet was a piece of a puzzle that was rapidly assembling itself into a disturbing picture of calculated malice and deep-seated resentment. The armadillo, Rio Seco's beloved mascot, wasn't just stolen; it was a pawn in a game of public humiliation, a symbol of the town's vulnerability. And the cryptic clues – the iridescent feather, the humming crate – hinted at something far more complex, a layer of the plot that Elme was only beginning to fathom. She clutched the plastic bag containing the evidence, her mind already racing, formulating a plan to expose the truth before the county fair became a stage for widespread embarrassment. She knew she had to act fast, to find a way to convince the authorities of the gravity of the situation, and that meant needing more than just hastily scribbled notes.

Suddenly, a scraping sound echoed from the main entrance of the mill, a jarring interruption to the tense silence. Esme froze, her heart leaping into her throat. Footsteps. Heavy, deliberate footsteps, crunching on the gravel outside and then on the decaying floorboards within. They were back. The perpetrators, whoever they were, had returned. A wave of adrenaline surged through her, sharpening her senses. She wasn't alone anymore, and the fragile stillness of the mill had been shattered by their unwelcome arrival.

Her skates, usually her silent companions in exploration, now felt like a liability, their whirring a siren's call in the echoing vastness of the mill. She ducked behind a stack of rusted barrels, the cold metal pressing against her cheek as she peered through a gap. Two figures emerged from the shadows, silhouetted against the weak moonlight filtering through the grimy windows. One was tall and broad-shouldered, unmistakably the 'stranger' she'd glimpsed in Finn's footage, his movements economical and purposeful. The other was shorter, his gait more agitated, his head swiveling nervously, taking in their surroundings. Danny, perhaps? Or the disgruntled former resident himself? The dim light and the sheer speed of the events made identification impossible, but their presence was undeniable, and their purpose clear: to retrieve whatever they had left behind.

Esme's breath hitched. She was trapped, caught in the heart of their operation, with the damning evidence clutched in her hand. Panic threatened to engulf her, but a steely resolve began to solidify within her. This was it, the confrontation Finn had warned her about. She couldn't let them get away with this. Not after coming this far, not after understanding the depth of their plan.

With a silent prayer, she shifted her weight, her skates finding purchase on the slick concrete. She needed to move, to create a diversion, to escape. As the two figures began to move deeper into the mill, their voices a low murmur of hushed urgency, Esme seized her opportunity. Pushing off from the barrels with a burst of speed, she shot out into the main space, her skates a blur of motion.

"Hey!" she yelled, her voice surprisingly steady, cutting through the oppressive gloom.

Both figures spun around, startled by her sudden appearance. The taller one, the stranger, moved with an unnerving swiftness, his hand reaching inside his jacket. The shorter one, momentarily stunned, recovered quickly, his eyes widening in disbelief and then narrowing with anger.

The chase was on.

Esme weaved through the labyrinthine layout of the mill, her skates a formidable advantage on the relatively smooth concrete floors. She zipped past towering piles of debris, ducked under precariously balanced beams, and skidded around support pillars. The roar of her skates was a desperate symphony, a desperate plea for attention, a signal to anyone who might be within earshot.

The stranger was relentless, his longer strides eating up the distance. He was strong, powerful, but Esme had agility and an intimate knowledge of the mill's layout, gleaned from her initial exploration. She used the environment to her advantage, forcing him to navigate obstacles that slowed his pursuit. She slid under a low-hanging conveyor belt, her body scraping against the dusty metal, and emerged on the other side, the stranger forced to stoop and grunt as he followed.

The shorter figure, seemingly less athletic, struggled to keep pace, his exasperated shouts echoing behind her. Esme risked a glance back. They were gaining, but she was still ahead. She could see the large opening of the loading dock, a sliver of moonlight beckoning her towards freedom.

Her path was blocked by a large, overturned forklift, its massive tines jutting out like a metallic monster. She couldn't go around it without losing precious seconds. Taking a deep breath, she crouched, her muscles coiling, and launched herself upwards. She soared over the forklift, landing with a jarring thud on the other side, her knees absorbing the impact. The effort sent a jolt through her, but the adrenaline was a powerful anesthetic.

The stranger, however, didn't attempt the jump. Instead, he let out a frustrated roar and veered off to the side, disappearing into a darker section of the mill. Esme's heart hammered against her ribs. Had she lost him? Or was he attempting a flanking maneuver?

She didn't have time to ponder. The shorter figure was still behind her, his breath coming in ragged gasps. As she rounded a corner, she saw it – the armadillo itself, its metallic shell gleaming faintly in the gloom, partially disassembled, lying beside the reinforced crate. It was still here, just as she had left it.

This was her chance. She skidded to a halt beside the mascot, her gloved hands reaching out to steady herself against its cool, smooth surface. The shorter man, seeing her intention, let out a bellow of rage and lunged.

But Esme was ready. As he closed in, she dropped to the floor, her skates allowing her to spin away from his grasp. She then used the armadillo's massive frame as a shield, a solid barrier between her and her pursuer. She could hear the stranger re-emerging from the shadows, his heavy footsteps now closing in from the other side. She was caught between them.

In that crucial moment, as both men converged, Esme reached into the pocket of her jacket and pulled out a small, high-pitched emergency whistle. She'd brought it for her own safety, a precaution that now felt like a lifeline.

She blew into it with all her might. The sound was piercing, shrill, a sharp, insistent shriek that sliced through the night air and reverberated through the derelict structure. It was a sound designed to carry, to cut through the usual quietude of Rio Seco, to alert anyone within earshot that something was terribly wrong.

The effect was immediate. The two men froze, their aggressive postures faltering. The stranger's head snapped towards the sound, his eyes narrowing with an even greater urgency. The shorter man, visibly panicked, looked towards the loading dock, his gaze darting as if seeking an escape route.

"The whistle!" the shorter man yelled, his voice tight with fear. "She's trying to alert someone!"

The stranger didn't respond verbally. Instead, he lunged, not at Esme, but towards the armadillo. His intention was clear: to silence her, to reclaim the mascot, and to escape before anyone arrived.

But Esme was no longer just fleeing. She had created the diversion, and now she had to stand her ground. As the stranger reached for the armadillo, she threw herself forward, not to protect the mascot itself, but to impede his progress. She slammed her shoulder into his side, a surprisingly effective move that threw him off balance. He stumbled, his massive frame rocking precariously.

In that instant, Esme saw her chance to retrieve her evidence, to make her escape, and to ensure that the town knew what was happening. She couldn't physically stop these men, but she could ensure their plan was exposed.

She turned and sprinted towards the loading dock, her skates a whirlwind of motion. The whistle was still clutched in her hand. She blew it again, a series of sharp, urgent blasts, each one a declaration of defiance. She could hear shouts behind her, the sound of pursuit resuming, but the whistle had done its job. Lights flickered on in the houses bordering the mill. Voices, startled and questioning, began to drift on the night air.

As she reached the edge of the loading dock, she risked one last look back. The two men were visible in the faint light, silhouetted against the interior gloom, their faces etched with fury and a dawning realization that their operation was compromised. The stranger seemed to be arguing with the shorter man, who was gesturing wildly towards the mill entrance.

Esme didn't wait to see more. She launched herself onto the ramp leading down from the dock, her skates carrying her forward with a surge of momentum. She hit the ground outside, the rough earth a welcome sensation beneath her wheels. She continued to skate, not stopping, not slowing, her lungs burning, the piercing sound of the whistle still echoing in her ears, a testament to her courage and her unwavering determination to protect her town. The confrontation had been terrifying, exhilarating, and ultimately, it had solidified her resolve. She had faced the darkness, and she had emerged, not unscathed, but unbroken, carrying the truth and a whistle that promised to shatter the silence of deception.

The rough concrete of the loading dock gave way to the uneven terrain of the unpaved road, a jarring transition that threatened to send Esme tumbling. But years of practice, of carving through skate parks and navigating city streets, had honed her instincts. Her skates, usually a whisper of movement, now roared a defiance against the pursuing footsteps echoing from the mill. The armadillo, surprisingly buoyant against her chest, felt like both a burden and a symbol of everything she was fighting for. Its metallic shell was cool against her racing heartbeat, a silent accomplice in her desperate flight.

She pushed off, the centrifugal force of her turn propelling her down the incline away from the abandoned building. The faint moonlight, which had seemed so meager inside the mill, now offered a patchy illumination of the path ahead. Twisted, skeletal trees clawed at the sky, their shadows stretching and contorting like monstrous fingers, adding to the disorienting nature of her escape. Her lungs burned with the effort, each breath a ragged gasp that did little to quench the fire within. Behind her, the guttural shouts of her pursuers were muffled by distance, but the steady thudding of their boots on the ground was a persistent reminder of the peril she was in.

The country road, a ribbon of dusty gray under the moon, twisted and turned with an almost malicious intent, designed to disorient and to trap. Esme, however, saw it as an opportunity. She knew these roads, had skated them a hundred times, memorizing every dip, every sharp bend, every patch of loose gravel. Her lime green skates, a beacon against the encroaching darkness, flashed with a frantic energy. She leaned into the turns, her body angled with practiced grace, the wheels of her skates biting into the earth, carrying her away from the clutches of the mill.

She could hear them now, their heavy breathing and the frantic scramble of their feet as they emerged from the mill's confines and onto the same road. They were faster on foot, no doubt, their longer strides an advantage on the open stretches. But the road wasn't always open. It snaked through dense patches of woods, where the trees pressed in, forcing her to rely on the fainter moonlight and her own honed spatial awareness. She used these denser sections to her advantage, her smaller frame and nimble skates allowing her to navigate the tighter turns and overhanging branches with a fluidity her pursuers couldn't match.

A particularly sharp bend loomed ahead, a near hairpin turn that dropped down a short, steep embankment. It was a section she usually tackled with caution, but now it was her only hope. She didn't hesitate. She launched herself into the turn, kicking out her leg to maintain balance, her skates digging in just enough to control her descent. She felt a jarring impact as she hit the bottom, the armadillo shifting precariously against her. She risked a glance back.

The taller of her pursuers, the one whose silent, predatory presence had unnerved her inside the mill, was attempting the turn. He was clearly not accustomed to the terrain, his powerful frame struggling to adapt to the uneven ground. He stumbled, a curse echoing through the trees, losing precious momentum. The shorter, more agitated man, however, seemed to be pushing himself with a desperate, almost manic energy, determined to close the gap.

Esme's mind raced, calculating distances, anticipating the path ahead. She knew the road would soon open up again, leading towards the outskirts of town. The sheriff's office was located on the edge of Rio Seco, near the old water tower. If she could reach that area, if she could create enough of a spectacle, enough noise, she might be able to draw attention. The whistle was still tucked safely in her pocket, a last resort. For now, she relied on the speed and agility her skates afforded her.

She skidded around another bend, the trees momentarily thinning to reveal a wider expanse of road. The armadillo, despite its bulk, was proving to be a surprisingly manageable passenger. She'd managed to wedge it securely against her chest, her arms wrapped around its metallic body, providing a semblance of stability. Its painted eyes, usually so cheerful, seemed to stare ahead blankly, as if mirroring her own determined, albeit terrified, focus.

She could hear them again, their voices closer now, laced with a desperate anger. "Get her!" the shorter one yelled, his voice hoarse. "Don't let her get away!"

Esme's calves burned, her quads screaming in protest. The adrenaline that had initially propelled her was starting to give way to sheer exhaustion. But the thought of what they had planned for the county fair, the humiliation they intended to inflict upon Rio Seco, fueled her resolve. She couldn't let them succeed. She wouldn't.

The road began to level out, the trees receding to reveal the familiar silhouette of the town's water tower against the bruised pre-dawn sky. Lights were starting to flicker on in the scattered houses that dotted the landscape on the outskirts of Rio Seco. Her whistle was a heavy weight in her pocket, a promise of a louder, more disruptive alarm if needed. But for now, she focused on her skating, on maintaining her speed, on putting as much distance between herself and her pursuers as possible.

She spotted a familiar landmark – Mrs. Gable's prize-winning petunias, meticulously arranged in a vibrant display along her garden path. They were a splash of color in the dim light, a sign that she was nearing civilization, nearing help. She also saw it then – a faint glimmer of blue and red flashing in the distance,

originating from the direction of the sheriff's office. The commotion, her whistle, perhaps even the distant shouts of her pursuers, had been heard. The sheriff was on his way.

A surge of hope, potent and exhilarating, coursed through her. She pushed harder, her skates gliding over the smoother asphalt of the town's edge. The sound of pursuit behind her was still present, but it seemed to be faltering, the pursuers likely realizing they were nearing a more populated area.

She could see the sheriff's cruiser now, its lights pulsing rhythmically, a beacon of safety in the gathering light.

She aimed for it, her trajectory unwavering. As she neared the cruiser, she heard the distinct sound of the sheriff's car door opening. Sheriff Brody, a man whose gruff exterior hid a deep well of kindness and dedication to his town, stepped out, his hand already resting on his holster, his eyes scanning the approaching darkness.

Esme's breath hitched. She was almost there. She could see the hulking shape of the armadillo in her arms, a bizarre and undeniable piece of evidence. She was nearing the sheriff, nearing salvation, but her pursuers were still close enough to pose a threat. She needed to make sure they didn't escape before the sheriff could intercept them.

With a final burst of energy, she steered her skates directly towards the sheriff's vehicle, weaving slightly to draw the sheriff's attention to her immediate surroundings. She could hear the scrabble of her pursuers' feet closing in behind her, the desperation in their movements palpable. She needed to be quick.

She skidded to a halt a few feet away from Sheriff Brody, her skates digging into the asphalt, sending up a small cloud of dust. The armadillo was still held tightly against her chest. She was panting, her entire body trembling with exertion and residual fear, but her eyes were locked on the sheriff.

"Sheriff!" she gasped, her voice raspy. "They're right behind me! They stole the armadillo! They… they were in the old mill!"

As if on cue, the two figures emerged from the gloom, their forms now more clearly defined against the flashing lights of the cruiser. The taller man, his face set in a grim mask of determination, and the shorter, more frenzied man, his eyes darting nervously. They had clearly seen the sheriff and realized their escape was compromised.

Sheriff Brody's gaze shifted from Esme to the approaching men, his expression hardening. He had dealt with petty criminals before, but the intensity and desperation etched on these two men's faces suggested something far more significant than a simple prank.

"Hold it right there!" Sheriff Brody's voice boomed, clear and authoritative, cutting through the night air. He drew his sidearm, holding it steady but not aimed directly at them, a clear signal of his intent to apprehend, not to engage violently. "Rio Seco Sheriff's Department! Don't move!"

The shorter man, his face contorted in a mixture of panic and defiance, hesitated for a fraction of a second. He glanced at the taller man, as if seeking direction, then began to turn, a clear intention to flee. But the taller man, with a surprising surge of speed, grabbed the shorter man's arm, pulling him back and shaking his head. It was a silent, tense exchange, a decision being made in the split second of the sheriff's command.

The flashing lights of the cruiser cast long, dancing shadows across the road, illuminating the standoff. Esme, her skates still firmly planted, watched with a mixture of relief and apprehension. She had done it. She had escaped, she had brought the armadillo back, and she had alerted the sheriff. The chase had been terrifying, a desperate dance on the edge of disaster, but it had ended here, under the watchful eye of the law. The secrets of the old mill, and the men who sought to manipulate the town's beloved mascot, were about to be brought into the harsh light of day. She still held the crumpled notes in her pocket, a silent testament to the chilling details of their plan, a plan that was now unraveling thanks to her courage and a pair of lime green roller skates. The fate of the armadillo, and indeed the smooth running of the county fair, rested on Sheriff Brody's next move.

6: Resolution and Reflections

The first rays of dawn painted the sky in hues of rose and gold, a stark contrast to the bruised pre-dawn darkness that had enveloped Rio Seco just hours before. The air, usually still and quiet at this hour, vibrated with a nascent energy, a palpable buzz that seemed to emanate from the very heart of the town. Word, as it always did in a place like Rio Seco, had spread like wildfire. The armadillo was safe. Esme had saved it.

As the sun climbed higher, casting its warm glow over the sleepy streets, the townsfolk began to emerge. They came from their homes, drawn by an invisible current towards the town square. Whispers turned into excited chatter, then into outright exclamations of relief and admiration. Children, usually still nestled in their beds, were already being bundled into jackets, their faces alight with the promise of a morning unlike any other. The story of Esme's daring rescue, of the chase through the darkened outskirts, of the armadillo's safe return, was already becoming legend.

Esme, still feeling the lingering ache in her muscles and the residual tremor of adrenaline, laced up her familiar lime green skates. The rough edges of the laces felt like a second skin, a comforting familiarity after the chaos of the night. She gently secured the armadillo mascot, 'Armie,' as it was affectionately known, to the front of her skates. Its metallic shell, still bearing faint smudges from its ordeal, gleamed dully in the morning light. Its perpetually cheerful painted eyes seemed to hold a newfound wisdom, a silent testament to its adventure. It felt heavier now, not just in weight, but in significance. Armie wasn't just a mascot; he was a symbol, and last night, he had been in grave danger.

Skating towards the town square, Esme felt a knot of nerves tighten in her stomach. She wasn't used to being the center of attention, especially not this kind of attention. Her skateboarding, her daring stunts, had always been a private passion, a way to escape and to express herself. But this was different. This was for Rio Seco.

As she rounded the corner onto Main Street, the scene that greeted her stole her breath. The town square, usually a quiet expanse of park benches and the occasional wilting flower display, was alive with people. Every shopfront seemed to have a cluster of faces peering out, and the square itself was rapidly filling. A ripple of recognition spread through the crowd as they spotted her, a collective gasp followed by a thunderous wave of cheers.

"Esme! Esme!" The chant rose, a chorus of gratitude and admiration. People waved, clapped, and shouted her name. Even Sheriff Brody, his uniform crisp and his expression one of weary satisfaction, was there, standing near the flagpole, his gaze fixed on her. He gave her a nod, a small, almost imperceptible smile playing on his lips, a silent acknowledgement of her courage.

She skated into the heart of the square, her wheels humming a triumphant tune on the worn cobblestones. The cheers intensified, a joyous cacophony that washed over her, drowning out any lingering fear or self-doubt. It was overwhelming, humbling, and incredibly exhilarating. She felt a warmth spread through her, a feeling of belonging and pride she hadn't known she was missing.

Mrs. Gable, her face beaming, pushed her way to the front, clutching a bouquet of her prize-winning petunias. "Oh, Esme, dear!" she exclaimed, her voice thick with emotion. "You saved him! You saved Armie! We're all so proud of you!" She thrust the flowers into Esme's free hand, their vibrant colors a beautiful counterpoint to the armadillo's metallic sheen.

Mayor Thompson, a portly man with a booming laugh, joined them, clapping Esme heartily on the shoulder. "Young lady, you've done Rio Seco a tremendous service! The county fair… well, it would have been a disaster without Armie. You've secured our reputation, and you've shown us all what true bravery looks like."

He gestured towards the two men being led into the back of Sheriff Brody's cruiser, their faces sullen and defeated. "Thanks to you, these scoundrels won't be causing any more trouble."

Esme's gaze followed the mayor's, her eyes meeting those of the taller of the two men. He looked less imposing in the daylight, his earlier menace replaced by a grim resignation. He wouldn't meet her eye. The shorter man, however, glared, a flicker of resentment in his gaze, but it was quickly extinguished as Sheriff Brody gave him a stern look.

"They were planning to tamper with Armie, weren't they?" Esme asked Sheriff Brody, her voice still a little hoarse. "The notes I found… they were talking about making him 'unrecognizable' for the fair."

Sheriff Brody adjusted his hat. "That's right, Esme. They intended to deface him, make him look ridiculous. Their plan was to try and embarrass our town, to make us look like we couldn't even keep track of our own mascot. Petty, low-down stuff. But thanks to your quick thinking and bravery, their little scheme has been thoroughly thwarted." He glanced at the two men being secured in the patrol car. "We found evidence in the mill that corroborates everything you said. They confessed to their intention to steal Armie and cause a scene at the fairgrounds. They even admitted to trying to scare you off when you stumbled upon them."

The weight of the night's events settled upon Esme. It hadn't just been a chase; it had been a deliberate act of sabotage, aimed at undermining the spirit of their town. And she, with her skates and her courage, had been the one to stop it.

The celebrations continued throughout the morning. People brought out lemonade and pastries, sharing stories and laughter. Children took turns gently patting Armie's shell, their eyes wide with wonder. Esme found herself surrounded by her friends, her parents beaming with pride, and even some of the townsfolk she barely knew. They all wanted to thank her, to shake her hand, to tell her how grateful they were.

"You were so brave, Esme," her best friend, Maya, said, her voice filled with awe. "When you told us you were going after them, I was so scared. But you did it. You actually did it."

Esme smiled, a genuine, unforced smile. "I had to," she said softly. "Armie means too much to everyone here. And I couldn't let them ruin the fair."

The sheriff approached, holding out a small, crumpled piece of paper. "This was in the pocket of the taller one, Esme," he said. "It looks like a list of...

instructions. And it mentions your name specifically. They clearly weren't expecting you to be so resourceful."

Esme took the paper, her fingers tracing the smudged ink. It was a crude drawing of Armie, with various Xs and annotations marking parts of its body. Below it, scrawled in messy handwriting, were the words: 'Disfigure. Humiliate. Disappear.' It was chillingly clear. They had targeted her, too.

"They knew I was… a bit of a lone wolf," Esme mused, remembering the furtive glances she'd received from them at the mill. "They probably thought I'd be an easy target, or someone who wouldn't be believed."

"Well, they underestimated you, Esme," Sheriff Brody said, his tone firm. "They underestimated the spirit of Rio Seco, and they certainly underestimated you. You're a true hero."

The afternoon sun cast long shadows across the square, signaling the end of the impromptu celebration. As the crowd began to disperse, a sense of quiet contentment settled over the town. Armie was back, safe and sound, ready to lead the parade. The county fair would go on as planned, a testament to the town's resilience and the courage of one young girl on skates.

Esme, standing by the flagpole, watched as the last few people waved goodbye. The armadillo mascot sat before her, a silent, shiny sentinel. The events of the night felt both like a distant dream and a vivid, indelible memory. She had faced fear, pursued danger, and emerged victorious. The lime green skates, scuffed and worn from their extraordinary journey, felt like extensions of herself, symbols of her newfound strength and determination. She had saved Armie, and in doing so, she had discovered a part of herself she never knew existed. The quiet town of Rio Seco, often overlooked and underestimated, had a champion, and she skated. The resolution was complete, but the reflections, Esme knew, were just beginning. The feeling of accomplishment, the knowledge that she had made a difference, was a quiet hum beneath the surface of her everyday life, a reminder that even the most ordinary girl, on the most ordinary skates, could accomplish extraordinary things. The armadillo was home, and so, in a way, was she. She had always felt a little out of sync with the rest of the town, preferring the solitude of her skates to the often-mundane social interactions. But today, surrounded by the joyous faces of her community, she felt a profound sense of connection. The cheers, the smiles, the grateful pats on the back – they weren't just for saving the armadillo; they were for standing up, for refusing to let fear win, for embodying the very spirit of Rio Seco that Armie represented. It was a feeling that would linger long after the last echoes of the celebration faded, a quiet confidence that would carry her through whatever adventures lay ahead. The sun dipped lower, casting a golden hue over the town square, and Esme knew that this was a day she would never forget. The return of Armie was not just the recovery of a mascot; it was the reaffirmation of community, the triumph of courage, and the quiet, powerful story of a girl who dared to skate against the odds.

The dust had settled, quite literally, on the recent commotion in Rio Seco. The morning sun, no longer a beacon of alarm but a warm embrace, illuminated the town square where the remnants of the impromptu celebration still lingered – a few stray petunia petals, a forgotten lemonade pitcher, the faint, sweet scent of Mrs. Gable's baking. Esme, still clad in her now slightly grimy lime green skates, felt a strange sense of calm descend upon her, a quiet aftermath to the adrenaline-fueled night. The cheers and accolades from earlier had subsided, replaced by a more intimate hum of conversations, the murmurs of a town processing the extraordinary events that had unfolded.

Sheriff Brody, his usual stoic demeanor softened by a hint of exhaustion and pride, stood near his cruiser, the two figures he had apprehended earlier now secured within its confines. They were the architect of the night's chaos and his reluctant accomplice. The taller one, the stranger whose eyes had held a chilling, unreadable depth, was quiet, his gaze fixed on the dusty ground. The other, a local face Esme vaguely recognized from the outskirts of town, looked visibly shaken, his eyes darting nervously towards the assembled townsfolk, a flicker of something akin to regret playing on his features.

"They're being processed down at the county station," Sheriff Brody informed Esme, his voice a low rumble that carried easily in the quiet air. He held a small, official-looking notebook, flipping through its pages. "The stranger, Silas Croft, he's got a rap sheet for petty vandalism and theft, mostly targeting small towns with a bit of local charm to exploit. Seems he saw Rio Seco and our dear Armie as an easy mark. The plan was to deface Armie, make a spectacle of it, and then demand a 'ransom' for his return – a shamefully large sum, mind you – all to be paid before the county fair."

He paused, then glanced towards the accomplice, who flinched under his gaze. "As for our local boy, young Billy Jenkins," Sheriff Brody continued, his tone taking on a more explanatory edge, "he was… persuaded. Croft played on Billy's dissatisfaction, his feeling of being overlooked in town. Promised him a cut, a way to finally make his mark. But it seems Billy's conscience, or perhaps just his fear, got the better of him when he realized just how far Croft was willing to go."

Esme listened intently, the pieces clicking into place. The cryptic notes, the hushed conversations she'd overheard near the old mill – it all painted a clearer, albeit darker, picture than she'd initially imagined. It wasn't just about a prank gone wrong; it was a calculated attempt to extort and humiliate their entire community.

"So, he really intended to… disfigure Armie?" Esme asked, still a little incredulous at the sheer audacity of it. She looked at the armadillo mascot, its metallic shell now gleaming under the full sun, looking as cheerful and inanimate as ever. It seemed almost impossible to fathom that something so innocent could have been the target of such malice.

"That was the plan," Sheriff Brody confirmed grimly. "The notes we found at the mill, the ones you pointed out – they were detailed instructions. Spray paint, permanent markers, even plans to attach some gaudy, cheap decorations that would have made Armie look… well, less than honorable, for lack of a better word. Croft wanted to ruin our town's pride, our mascot, just before the fair. A twisted way of getting back at a world he felt had wronged him, I suppose."

He then turned his attention to Billy Jenkins, who was now being escorted to the passenger side of the cruiser by a deputy. "Billy," Sheriff Brody called out, his voice firm but not unkind. "You did the right thing by talking to Esme, by trying to warn her, even if you were too scared to come forward yourself. Your cooperation now, after the fact, it matters. It helps us make sure people like Croft don't get away with this kind of behavior again."

Billy mumbled something inaudible, his face a picture of mortification. Esme felt a pang of something akin to sympathy. He had been a pawn, manipulated and coerced, and his fear had likely outweighed his loyalty to his community.

The crowd, which had ebbed and flowed throughout the morning, now seemed to coalesce around Esme again. Her parents, Maya, and a handful of other friends had stayed close, their presence a quiet anchor. Mrs. Gable, her face still beaming, approached Esme once more, this time with a plate of freshly baked cookies.

"Oh, Esme, dear," she said, her voice warm and comforting. "You were so brave. So very brave. I overheard the Sheriff. It sounds like it was all quite... serious." She looked at Esme with a mixture of admiration and concern. "I, for one, apologize for ever doubting you. When you first mentioned something felt off, and then you went out on your skates… well, I confess, I worried you were being a bit fanciful. But you were right, weren't you? You saw what others couldn't, or wouldn't."

Esme shook her head, accepting a cookie. "It's okay, Mrs. Gable. I wouldn't have done anything differently. I just wish… I wish Billy hadn't gotten mixed up in it."

"He'll learn from this," Mayor Thompson chimed in, stepping closer. He placed a hand on Esme's shoulder, his grip firm and reassuring. "And so will we all. We tend to get complacent, you know. We see our town as peaceful, predictable. We forget that sometimes, danger lurks in the quietest of places. But you, Esme, you reminded us. You showed us that courage isn't about not being afraid; it's about doing what's right, even when you are afraid. And you did that, magnificently."

He gestured towards the cruiser again, where Billy Jenkins was now seated. "And to think," the Mayor continued, his voice dropping slightly, "that it was one of our own who was involved… it's a sobering thought. But as Sheriff Brody said, his cooperation is valuable. He'll have to face the consequences, of course, but perhaps this experience will steer him onto a better path. A path where he understands the importance of community, of honesty, rather than being swayed by the empty promises of outsiders."

Esme looked at Billy, really looked at him, and saw not a criminal, but a scared young man who had made a terrible mistake. She remembered her own moments of doubt, her own feelings of being an outsider, and she understood, on a fundamental level, how someone like Croft could exploit those vulnerabilities.

"I… I want to apologize too, Esme," came a hesitant voice from nearby. It was Maya. Esme turned, surprised. Maya was rarely shy, but Esme could tell this was difficult for her.

"What for, Maya?" Esme asked gently.

"For… for not taking you more seriously earlier," Maya admitted, her cheeks flushing slightly. "When you first told us about the strange car, and the men near the mill, I brushed it off. I thought you were just seeing things, or getting too caught up in one of your adventurous moods. I should have listened more, believed you more. I'm really sorry, Esme."

Esme's heart ached with affection for her friend. "Oh, Maya. Don't be sorry. We're all friends. And honestly, I wasn't entirely sure myself. It was all so strange. You were just being a good friend, worrying about me." She gave Maya a small, reassuring smile. "But thanks for saying that. It means a lot."

The conversations continued, a tapestry of explanations, apologies, and shared relief. The townsfolk, no longer a frenzied mob but a community united by a shared experience, continued to approach Esme, their words a chorus of gratitude. Some offered her money, which she politely declined. Others offered her baked goods or promises of future favors. Most simply looked at her with newfound respect, their eyes reflecting the quiet admiration that had replaced the earlier awe.

Esme, usually more comfortable in the solitude of her skates, found herself the unexpected center of a town's collective affection. It was a strange sensation, this public validation of her quiet pursuits. Her skating, her keen observation skills, her willingness to act – things she'd always considered personal quirks – had proven to be valuable assets, not just to herself, but to Rio Seco.

Sheriff Brody, as he prepared to drive away with his prisoners, called out to her one last time. "Esme, you did a remarkable job. If you ever need anything, or if you ever see anything that doesn't seem right, you know where to find me. Rio Seco is lucky to have you."

With a final nod, the cruiser pulled away, the flashing lights a fading beacon in the bright afternoon sun. The crowd began to thin out, the townsfolk returning to their homes, their shops, their everyday lives, but with a subtle shift in their perspective. The incident had woven itself into the fabric of Rio Seco's history, a testament to resilience and unexpected heroism.

Esme remained in the square for a while longer, the armadillo mascot now safely secured in the back of her parents' car. She traced the scuff marks on her skates, remnants of her nighttime adventure. The thrill of the chase, the fear, the exhilaration — it all felt like a dream, yet the quiet satisfaction of knowing she had made a difference was a very real, grounding sensation.

She watched as Mayor Thompson, Sheriff Brody, and a few other town leaders gathered near the flagpole, discussing the finer points of securing Armie for the fair, making sure such an incident would never be repeated. Their serious expressions were underscored by a shared sense of purpose, a quiet determination to protect their town.

A sense of peace settled over Esme. The loose ends had been unraveled, the mystery solved, and the culprits apprehended. The explanations had been given, the motivations understood, and the apologies offered, both spoken and unspoken. She had played her part, not with a grand pronouncement, but with quiet action, with the courage born from a genuine love for her town and its quirky, beloved mascot.

As the sun began its slow descent, casting long, golden shadows across the square, Esme knew that while the immediate crisis was over, her perspective had irrevocably shifted. She was no longer just the girl who skated; she was the girl who had saved Armie, the girl who had faced down danger and emerged victorious. And in the quiet reflection of that realization, amidst the fading echoes of cheers and the gentle hum of a town returning to its peaceful rhythm, Esme felt a profound sense of belonging, a quiet pride that settled deep within her, as warm and comforting as the late afternoon sun. The adventure had ended, but the story, her story, was just beginning to truly unfold. She had unraveled the knots of mystery, and in doing so, she had also begun to unravel the complexities of her own place within the heart of Rio Seco.

The familiar chime of the Sonic's bell was a symphony Esme had always found comforting, a soundtrack to the predictable ebb and flow of Rio Seco's daily life. Now, however, it seemed to carry a different cadence, a subtle note of acknowledgment that vibrated beneath the usual cheerful din. Back behind the counter, clad in her familiar red Sonic uniform, the scent of fried onions and sweet, creamy milkshakes a welcome perfume, Esme felt a curious blend of the ordinary and the extraordinary. The adrenaline of the past night had long since dissipated, replaced by a quiet satisfaction that settled deep in her bones, as reassuring as the worn leather of her roller skates.

"Hey, Esme!" A voice, bright and familiar, cut through the gentle hum of conversation. It was Mrs. Gable, beaming as she approached the counter, a half-eaten apple pie peeking out from a checkered bag. "Just wanted to pick up another root beer float. My grandkids are visiting, you see, and they insisted on trying the float that our little hero makes!"

Esme felt a blush creep up her neck, a warmth that had nothing to do with the grill. "Of course, Mrs. Gable. Coming right up." As she expertly scooped the ice cream and poured the fizzy root beer, she met the elder woman's gaze. There was no hint of the past suspicion in her eyes, only genuine warmth and admiration. It was a look Esme was seeing more and more of these days, a silent testament to the night's events.

"You know," Mrs. Gable continued, leaning conspiratorially over the counter, "when you first started talking about all those oddities, I'll admit, I thought you might be getting a bit too imaginative with your skating tales. But you, my dear, you were right all along. You saw what no one else did." She patted Esme's hand, her touch gentle and firm. "And you handled it all with such… such bravery. We're all so proud of you."

Esme offered a shy smile, handing over the frothy concoction. "Thank you, Mrs. Gable. It was… an experience." An understatement, to be sure, but one that captured the surreal nature of it all. The whispers and curious glances she'd received earlier in the morning had gradually transformed into open smiles and words of gratitude. She was no longer just the quiet girl who skated through town; she was Esme, the one who had, in her own unassuming way, saved Armie.

As Mrs. Gable departed, the next customer approached. It was Mr. Henderson, the owner of the hardware store, a man usually gruff and preoccupied with inventory. Today, however, his face was creased with a warm smile. "Morning, Esme. One large chocolate shake, please. And make it a double for me." He winked. "Heard you were quite the detective last night. Keeping Rio Seco safe, one set of wheels at a time."

"Just doing my part, Mr. Henderson," Esme replied, her hands moving with practiced ease, assembling the milkshake. She still felt a thrill of her own competence, a quiet confidence that had blossomed in the wake of the crisis. Her keen eye for detail, her ability to connect seemingly unrelated observations, traits she'd always cultivated through her solitary explorations, had proven to be more than just personal quirks. They were tools, valuable ones, that had helped preserve the town's cherished mascot and its innocent reputation.

The day unfolded in a similar fashion, a steady stream of familiar faces, each offering a word of encouragement or a simple, appreciative nod. The usual rush of lunchtime brought a flurry of orders, the clatter of trays, and the sizzle of burgers on the grill, a comforting symphony of normalcy. Yet, woven into this familiar rhythm was a new thread of connection. Esme found herself engaging in conversations that went beyond the usual transactional pleasantries. People asked about her skating, about her observations, their curiosity genuine, their respect palpable.

"You know, Esme," a young woman named Sarah, who worked at the bakery, said as she collected her order, "I always admired how you seemed to know everything that was going on in town, just by skating around. I figured you just had a knack for gossip, but now I see it was real observation. You're amazing."

Esme laughed softly. "I just like to pay attention, I guess." It was true. She found a peculiar joy in observing the subtle shifts in people's moods, the unspoken dramas playing out in the quiet corners of Rio Seco. Her skates were her vantage point, allowing her to see the town from a unique perspective, to notice the nuances that others might overlook. And now, it seemed, her quiet passion had finally been recognized, not as an eccentricity, but as a strength.

Even Maya, her best friend, seemed to carry a different energy around Esme. The apology Maya had offered earlier, sincere and heartfelt, had smoothed over any lingering awkwardness. Now, Maya was openly proud, often recounting Esme's bravery to their mutual friends with an enthusiasm that made Esme a little shy.

"Seriously, Esme," Maya said, leaning against the counter during a brief lull, her eyes sparkling, "I still can't believe you outsmarted those guys. I mean, the way you put it all together, the notes, the car… it was like something out of a movie! You're like a real-life Nancy Drew, but cooler, because you skate."

Esme nudged her playfully. "Don't exaggerate, Maya. It was mostly luck and a bit of luck." But she couldn't deny the quiet satisfaction that surged through her at her friend's genuine admiration. It was a different kind of validation than the thrill of a successful skate, a deeper, more resonant feeling of belonging.

The aroma of coffee brewing, the hiss of the milkshake machine, the murmur of conversations — it all coalesced into a familiar and comforting sensory tapestry. Esme moved through her shifts with a newfound ease. The routine, which had sometimes felt mundane, now offered a sense of grounding. It was a reminder that even after extraordinary events, life continued, and her place within it was secure, perhaps even more so than before.

Sheriff Brody stopped by during his afternoon patrol, his presence commanding yet friendly. He ordered a burger and fries, his eyes twinkling as he watched Esme work. "Still can't get over it, Esme," he said, his voice a low rumble that carried a hint of genuine amusement. "The town's hero, serving up burgers. You know, some folks are talking about giving you a key to the city. Or at least, free milkshakes for life."

Esme blushed again. "That's very kind, Sheriff, but I'm happy right here." And she was. The excitement of the chase had been exhilarating, but the quiet satisfaction of returning to her familiar surroundings, of being recognized for her unique contributions, was even more rewarding. She understood now, more than ever, the importance of community, of the shared values that bound Rio Seco together. Her actions had protected not just a metal armadillo, but the very spirit of the town.

The sunlight streamed through the windows of the
Sonic, casting golden bars across the checkered floor.
Esme wiped down a table, her movements efficient and
practiced. She still noticed the small details – the way
the light caught the dust motes dancing in the air, the
subtle shift in the aroma of the fries as they cooled, the
quiet camaraderie between her coworkers. These were
the observations that had always fueled her, that had
made her feel connected to the pulse of the town, even
when she felt like an outsider. Now, those same
observations felt like an affirmation, a confirmation of
her place.

She thought back to the night before, the rush of fear,
the adrenaline, the sheer terror of facing the unknown.
It felt like a distant memory, a vivid dream that had
somehow bled into reality. But the aftermath, this quiet
appreciation, this newfound respect – that was real. It
was a tangible shift in the way people saw her, and
more importantly, the way she saw herself. She was still
the girl on skates, still the girl who loved to observe,
but now she was also the girl who had stepped up, who
had made a difference.

As the afternoon wore on, the sun began its slow
descent, painting the sky in hues of orange and pink.
The familiar sounds of the Sonic continued, a
comforting, constant presence. Esme caught her
reflection in the polished surface of the milkshake

machine – her uniform slightly rumpled, a smudge of ketchup on her cheek, her eyes bright with a quiet confidence. She was back to her ordinary life, serving familiar treats to familiar faces. But nothing, she realized, was truly ordinary anymore. She had found her voice, her courage, and her place, not just on the streets of Rio Seco, but within the heart of its community. The clatter of trays, the scent of fries, the sweet chime of the bell – it was all more comforting, more resonant, than ever before. It was home, and she was, finally, truly, a part of it.

The familiar rhythm of the Sonic was a balm, a steady beat beneath the hum of conversations and the sizzle of the grill. Esme moved through the afternoon rush, her movements fluid and practiced, yet imbued with a new sense of purpose. The lingering scent of fried onions and sweet, creamy milkshakes still clung to her uniform, a comforting anchor to the ordinary. But beneath the surface of this comfortable routine, a profound shift had occurred. The adrenaline of the previous night had faded, replaced by a quiet, deep-seated knowing. She was no longer just Esme, the girl who served shakes and skates through town. She was Esme, the one who had seen, the one who had understood, the one who had acted.

Mrs. Gable's genuine admiration, Mr. Henderson's surprised wink, Sarah's enthusiastic praise, even Maya's unbridled pride – each interaction was a tiny ripple in the pond of her perception. They saw her differently now, yes, but more importantly, she was beginning to see herself differently. For so long, her keen eye for detail, her tendency to notice the minutiae that others skimmed over, had felt like an inherent part of her, as natural as breathing. She'd always been the observer, the one who absorbed the subtle currents of Rio Seco, the unspoken dramas playing out in quiet corners. Her skates, her constant companions, were the conduits for this immersion. They allowed her to glide through the town, a silent witness to its many facets, to its people, its rhythms, its secrets.

She remembered the countless hours spent tracing the worn asphalt paths, the dusty trails, the quiet residential streets. Each glide was an exploration, not just of the physical landscape, but of the social one. She'd learned the cadence of the school bell, the schedules of the delivery trucks, the preferred routes of the town's residents, the familiar patterns of their daily lives. These weren't just idle observations; they were the building blocks of her understanding. She'd learned to read the subtle cues – a hurried step, a lingering glance, a hushed conversation snatched from the air. These were the threads that wove the tapestry of Rio Seco, and she had an intimate familiarity with every strand.

There were times, of course, when this heightened awareness felt like a burden. In a world that often valued speed and efficiency, her inclination to pause, to observe, to analyze, could feel out of sync. She'd sometimes catch herself being drawn into the intricate details of a scene, losing track of time, only to realize she was miles off her intended path. She'd been teased, gently, by Maya for her "Molesworth-like attention to detail," a playful jab that, at the time, had stung a little. She'd wondered if this constant internal monologue, this ceaseless processing of sensory input, was a sign of something wrong, a disconnect from the more straightforward way most people experienced the world.

But last night, that very inclination, that very way of *being*, had been her greatest asset. The cryptic notes, the unusual car parked down by the old mill, the peculiar behavior of the man claiming to be a tourist – these weren't random occurrences to Esme. They were anomalies in the familiar pattern, dissonances that immediately set off her internal alarm. While others might have dismissed them as inconsequential, her mind, honed by years of silent observation, had cataloged them, cross-referenced them, and, crucially, connected them.

The sheer terror of the situation had been undeniable. The cold dread that had gripped her as she'd pieced together the fragments of information had been a visceral reminder of her vulnerability. Yet, even in that fear, her observational instincts had remained sharp. She'd noticed the brand of the cigarette butt, the specific model of the car, the almost imperceptible tremor in the man's hand as he'd spoken. These details, seemingly insignificant to anyone else, had been the very keys that unlocked the mystery. Her skates, the very means by which she'd navigated her world, had also been her escape route, her silent wings that carried her from danger and allowed her to relay her findings.

This realization settled over her like a warm blanket. Her perspective wasn't a flaw; it was her superpower. Her skates weren't just a mode of transport; they were her mobile observation deck, her personal amphitheater from which to view the intricate workings of Rio Seco. They allowed her to approach life with a unique blend of detachment and immersion. She could be a part of the town, gliding through its streets, yet also maintain a critical distance, a clear-eyed view of its complexities.

She thought about Armie, the town's beloved, if slightly dilapidated, metal armadillo mascot. For weeks, there had been whispers, theories, and a general sense of unease about its sudden disappearance. The police had conducted their inquiries, the community had expressed its concern, but the trail had gone cold, swallowed by the vastness of assumption and misdirection. Esme, however, had simply continued her patrols. She'd seen the man with the van, noted the unfamiliar license plate, observed the hushed exchange near the abandoned warehouse. These were not pieces of a puzzle that presented themselves neatly; they were fragments scattered across the town, revealed only to someone willing to look, willing to connect the dots that lay hidden in plain sight.

The man who'd claimed to be a tourist, his accent just a shade too perfect, his knowledge of local landmarks eerily rehearsed – he was a red flag that only she had seemed to register. The way he'd lingered near the town square, his eyes not taking in the picturesque scenery, but scanning, calculating. Esme had seen him before, on her usual routes, always in the periphery, always a fleeting glimpse. But that night, his presence had been too deliberate, too out of place, to ignore. Her mind had filed away the details of his vehicle, the peculiar way he'd seemed to be mapping out the town, and when Armie had vanished, those stored observations had suddenly snapped into focus.

It wasn't a sudden flash of brilliance, but a slow, methodical piecing together, much like assembling a complex jigsaw puzzle. The car she'd seen near the mill, the one matching the description of the man's vehicle, had been parked in a spot where it shouldn't have been, out of the usual flow of traffic. The hushed conversation she'd overheard near the old railway tracks, the furtive exchange of a bulky object — it all began to make a grim kind of sense. And her skates, her silent partners in this endeavor, had allowed her to cover ground quickly, to verify her suspicions, to follow the faint trail that the perpetrators had left behind.

This journey had been more than just a rescue mission; it had been a profound validation of her inner world. The quiet confidence that now resided within her was different from the fleeting thrill of mastering a new skate trick or the satisfaction of a perfectly executed turn. This was a deeper, more resonant sense of self-worth. It was the understanding that her way of experiencing the world, the very things she had sometimes felt insecure about, were not only valid but essential. They were the tools that had allowed her to contribute, to protect, to make a tangible difference in the lives of the people she cared about.

The smiles and nods she'd received throughout the day weren't just acknowledgments of her bravery; they were also, she suspected, acknowledgments of her unique perception. People were starting to see the value in her quiet observation, in her independent spirit. They recognized that her solitary patrols weren't a sign of aloofness, but a dedication to understanding the fabric of their community.

Maya's words, "You're like a real-life Nancy Drew, but cooler, because you skate," echoed in her mind. It was a playful comparison, but it held a kernel of truth. Nancy Drew, like Esme, was an avid observer, a tenacious investigator who relied on her sharp intellect and her willingness to look where others wouldn't. The addition of the skates, however, added a dimension Maya had instinctively grasped — a unique freedom, a mobility, a perspective that set Esme apart. Her skates weren't just a way to get around; they were an extension of her curiosity, a tool that allowed her to explore the world on her own terms.

The afternoon sun, now beginning its slow descent, cast long shadows across the Sonic's checkered floor. Esme paused for a moment, leaning against the cool metal of the milkshake machine, watching the ebb and flow of customers. She saw the subtle shifts in their expressions, the unconscious gestures that revealed their inner states, the way they interacted with each other. These were the details she had always absorbed, the language she had always understood. Now, it felt different. It felt like she was not just observing, but participating, her understanding serving as a bridge, connecting her more deeply to the community.

She thought about the feeling of being an outsider, a sensation that had sometimes accompanied her solitary journeys. While she loved her town, there were moments when she felt like a spectator, watching life unfold from a slight distance. But last night had irrevocably altered that perception. By stepping out of the periphery and into the heart of a crisis, she had forged a new connection, a stronger bond with Rio Seco. Her actions had demonstrated that her unique perspective wasn't a barrier to belonging, but a pathway to it. She had protected Armie, yes, but in doing so, she had also protected the shared innocence and trust that defined their small town.

The day at the Sonic was drawing to a close, the usual after-school crowd starting to trickle in. Esme tied her apron a little tighter, a small smile playing on her lips. The scent of fries, the clatter of dishes, the murmur of voices – it was all familiar, comforting. But within this familiar setting, Esme felt a profound transformation. Her adventure had not only brought Armie back to his rightful place, but it had also brought Esme into a clearer understanding of herself and her place in the world. Her independent spirit, her keen observation, her trusty skates – they were not just facets of her personality, but essential instruments that had allowed her to navigate a crisis and emerge with a newfound sense of purpose and belonging. The path ahead, she realized, would be less about fitting in and more about embracing the unique way she experienced the world, a perspective that had proven to be her greatest strength. She was still Esme, the girl who loved to skate, but now she was also Esme, the girl who saw, the girl who understood, the girl who made a difference. The reflection in the milkshake machine's polished surface showed a smudge of ketchup on her cheek, her eyes bright with a quiet, unwavering confidence. The ordinary had become extraordinary, and she was ready for whatever came next, her skates poised for the journey.

The late afternoon sun, a smear of molten gold across the bruised purple sky, seemed to beckon Esme forward. She stood at the edge of town, her skates glinting in the fading light, a familiar ache of anticipation thrumming in her veins. Rio Seco, with its quiet streets and predictable rhythms, had always been her world, but lately, that world felt both smaller and infinitely larger. The adventure of the past few weeks, the thrill of uncovering secrets and the quiet satisfaction of making a difference, had cracked open her perception of what was possible. The girl who'd once dreamt of escaping the confines of her small town now found herself looking at it with new eyes, seeing not limitations, but the deep, intricate threads of connection that bound her to its very soul.

The memory of the frantic chase, the chill of fear, and the surge of adrenaline was still a vivid imprint on her senses. Yet, it was no longer a haunting specter. Instead, it was a testament to her own resilience, a quiet reminder that she possessed a strength she'd never acknowledged. She remembered the sheer, unadulterated joy of seeing Armie, safe and sound, perched on the back of the police car, his metallic grin somehow radiating relief. The cheers of the townspeople, the relieved sighs of her parents, Maya's ecstatic hug – these were moments etched into the fabric of her being, moments that whispered of potential and courage. She'd always been the observer, the one who noticed the small details, the quiet nuances. Now, she understood that observation wasn't passive; it was an active force, capable of shaping reality, of protecting what was precious.

Her skates, her trusty steeds, felt different beneath her feet. They were no longer just a means of getting from one place to another, or a way to escape awkward conversations. They were extensions of herself, tools of discovery, instruments of freedom. As she pushed off from the cracked pavement, gliding towards the open road that led away from Rio Seco, a familiar yearning tugged at her. The world outside, with its bustling cities and endless horizons, still held its allure. She pictured herself in places she'd only read about in books, experiencing lives far removed from the quiet hum of her hometown. The thought of leaving, of shedding the skin of the familiar, was still a tempting prospect.

But as she skated, the wind whipping through her hair, a different kind of dream began to unfurl. It wasn't a dream of escape, but a dream of return, of bringing the experiences she would gather back to the place that had shaped her. She saw herself exploring new landscapes, learning new skills, challenging herself in ways she hadn't yet imagined. And then, she saw herself returning to Rio Seco, not as the girl who was eager to leave, but as the woman who had a story to tell, a perspective to share, and perhaps, a new way to contribute. Her skates, she realized, were the perfect vehicles for this dual journey — they could carry her to the farthest reaches of her imagination and bring her back, grounded and enriched.

The notion of "what's next" had always been a nebulous concept for Esme, a shimmering, uncertain future. Now, it felt more defined, less like a vast, uncharted territory and more like a series of paths, each with its own unique appeal. She could see herself as a journalist, using her keen observational skills to uncover hidden truths. Or perhaps an investigator, a real-life detective, solving mysteries that baffled others. The skills she had honed – her attention to detail, her ability to connect seemingly disparate pieces of information, her quiet persistence – were valuable, tangible assets. They weren't just quirks of her personality; they were the building blocks of a future, a future she was now actively creating.

She remembered the hushed conversations, the worried glances, the collective sigh of relief when Armie was found. It was a testament to the power of community, to the shared sense of belonging that existed in Rio Seco, even in its quietest moments. She hadn't acted alone in her investigation, not really. Maya's unwavering support, her parents' quiet trust, even the casual nods of recognition from townsfolk as she'd skated by – these were all part of the tapestry. Her adventure had woven her more tightly into that tapestry, transforming her from an observer on the fringes to an integral part of the whole.

The setting sun painted the clouds in hues of orange, pink, and fiery red, a spectacle that always made her pause. It was a reminder of the cyclical nature of life, of endings that paved the way for new beginnings. Her skates allowed her to witness these moments of transition, these ephemeral shifts in the world around her, with a unique intimacy. She could glide through the golden hour, the very air alive with the day's last warmth, and feel a profound sense of peace. This was not just about the thrill of adventure; it was about the quiet beauty of observation, the deep satisfaction of understanding the world in her own way.

The late 1970s were a time of change, of burgeoning independence for young women. Esme felt that shift in her bones, a sense of burgeoning possibility that mirrored the changing times. She was no longer content with simply accepting the world as it was presented to her. She wanted to understand it, to explore it, to contribute to it. Her roller skates were the embodiment of this spirit – they offered freedom, mobility, and a unique perspective. They allowed her to carve her own path, to defy expectations, to embrace the unknown with a mixture of trepidation and exhilaration.

She thought about Maya, her best friend, who was already talking about college, about cities far beyond Rio Seco. There was no doubt in Esme's mind that Maya would go, and she would thrive. And Esme? She would go too, eventually. But the urgency, the desperate need to escape, had faded. Now, it was a choice, a deliberate step towards a larger world, taken with the knowledge that she carried Rio Seco with her, its lessons and its love woven into her very being. Her skates would be her companions, carrying her through new experiences, always ready to glide her towards the next horizon.

The road ahead was still unwritten, a blank canvas waiting for her to fill it with her own unique strokes. But she wasn't afraid. The quiet confidence that had bloomed within her was a sturdy, resilient thing, nurtured by her experiences. She knew that no matter where her skates took her, she would always have her keen eyes, her observant mind, and her unwavering spirit. These were her true treasures, her constant companions, the things that would allow her to navigate any terrain, any challenge, any dream. The sun dipped lower, casting a long, warm glow that seemed to embrace her, a silent affirmation of the endless possibilities that lay before her, waiting to be discovered, one glide at a time. She took a deep breath, tasting the crisp evening air, and pushed off, her silhouette a bold, confident line against the fading light, a symbol of youth, adventure, and the boundless journey of self-discovery. The world was vast, and her skates were ready.

Rio Seco's Historic Roller Rink: Established in 1955, the Rio Seco Roller Rink was a beloved community hub, known for its polished wooden floor and dazzling disco ball. It closed its doors in 1981, a casualty of changing trends, but remains a fond memory for many long-time residents.

The Legend of the Sunstone Locket: Local folklore tells of a locket, crafted from a rare, sun-warmed stone, said to grant the wearer clarity and courage. While its existence has never been definitively proven, it has inspired generations of Rio Seco's young dreamers.

Gliding: The act of moving smoothly and continuously on roller skates.

Cracked pavement: The uneven, often damaged surface of roads or sidewalks, a familiar sight in many older towns.

Molten gold: Describing the intense, liquid-like color of the setting sun.

Bruised purple sky: The deep, dusky hues that can appear in the sky just before or after sunset.

Ephemeral shifts: Subtle, fleeting changes, often used to describe natural phenomena like light or weather.

Smith, J. (1978). The Roller Skating Revolution: Freedom on Wheels. Sports Illustrated Press.

Thompson, E. (1979). Small Town Secrets: Uncovering the Hidden Histories of America. University of Heartland Press.

Garcia, M. (1977). Chasing Horizons: A Young Woman's Guide to Exploration. Wanderlust Publications.